CALASPIA

A. D. MCLAIN

To my family for giving me the time to pursue my passion.

PROLOGUE
TWO-HUNDRED YEARS PREVIOUS

S he stood alone. Adeline looked longingly across the field at the nearby lake. A few more leagues, and she would be at the portal. Adeline felt queasy. Lately, she'd felt more comfortable there than at her own home. Why couldn't he leave her be? That man was obsessed. They weren't even the same kind. She was water. He was land. Why Gelick was fixated on her, she had no idea. It was downright creepy.

She stared at the reflection of the plum-tinged evening sun bouncing off the undisturbed water and wished for some solution to present itself. While she more than enjoyed her time on Earth, she couldn't continue to spend all her time there. Nor could she allow him to drive her away from her family and friends. Of course, that was easier said than done; even with her eel animal spirit, she still had a human side and needed to spend time outside the water. And though she was seriously testing all known limits for time spent in her eel-hybrid form, barely surfacing save for necessity, he always seemed to know when she would emerge. If she didn't know better, she'd say he camped near the water's perimeter in wait.

Adeline jumped when a hand grabbed her around the waist. Gelick smiled apologetically and stepped to the side. "Sorry to surprise you. How was your afternoon? I'd heard you visited those Earth lakes again. Are you sure you should be doing that? Things there have been getting increasingly dangerous for our kind."

Putting a few steps between them, Adeline turned to face him. Her skin crawled. It was bad enough he always found her here, but how could he possibly know of her travels through the portal? Somehow, he'd found a way to monitor her movements and activities. He took liberties that were not his to take!

She silently bid her brother to return home, but there was no way of knowing if he'd heard her. Bry was still back at the lake, and communication between Calaspia and Earth was difficult and sporadic. Some thoughts made it through, but it wasn't dependable. Even so, she sent the plea. In the meantime, she looked around for a way out. The water was a good hundred feet away. She could make a run for it, but he'd easily overtake her on the land before she ever made it.

She shook her head, wondering what was wrong with her. Okay, so he was creepy, but it wasn't like he'd hurt her. He seemed *legitimately* worried for her safety. Maybe he'd just overheard someone talking about her visits? He couldn't possibly be able to track her underwater. "I appreciate your concern, but the humans tend to stay away from the deep water, so there's little to worry about."

"If that's the case then, why do the villagers near the lake speak of strange serpentine lake creatures, my Naita-ka?" He whispered the name like an endearment.

Her eyes widened in surprise. He knew the name the humans had given for her and the others who traveled through to the other side. It was what they called their lake monster. She hadn't told anyone that. Neither had Bry. There was only one way he could have known about the rumors. "You've been to the village?"

"Of course." He stepped toward her with his arm outstretched. "I had to make sure you were safe, and I'm glad I did. If you continue to go there, they'll find you and possibly do you harm. You *must* stop these excursions."

Her eyes blazed with anger. "That's none of your concern."

"None of my concern? You *are* my concern!"

"No, I'm not," she said flatly.

His eyes flared feline for the briefest of moments. "It's Bry, isn't it? He's never approved of our relationship."

"We have no relationship!" she cried out in frustration.

Gelick's eyes softened, and he placed a hand gently on her arm. "I understand you're afraid, but there is no reason our kinds cannot be together."

He was insane. What else could she say to that? She couldn't think of any way to be clearer

"Let go of my sister," Bry's voice called out.

Gelick's fingers curled, his sharp nails digging painfully into her arm. She didn't flinch. The ache was nothing compared to the anger rolling off him, pressing against her until she could barely breathe.

Bry approached from the shore, water still dripping off his body. Heavy breathing indicated the speed with which he'd swam here. Gelick's eyes suddenly appeared feline. His lips curved up at the corners. She felt her heart in her throat.

"Bry, run!" She pulled her arm from his grasp, leaving

jagged, bloody scratches from her elbow to wrist, and took off for the water.

Mid run, Gelick transformed into his panther form, a sleek black beast of pure muscle and precision. On land, he had the advantage. They had no chance of outrunning him here. She caught Bry's eyes and felt time stop. He looked between her and Gelick, and then to the lake, and came to the same conclusion.

She skidded to a halt and watched as he turned toward the attack and braced for impact. "Get to the lake," he ordered, just as Gelick's powerful claws dug into his arm and shoulder.

They fell to the ground in a tumble of fur and limbs. Bry fought back, but he was no match for Gelick's stronger animal form. He had no claws and no protection, but he grabbed at the panther's mouth, trying to hold back his teeth; with minimal effort, he shook free of the hands. She screamed and ran back to them.

Gelick's razor-sharp teeth ripped Bry's flesh. Red splattered the grass and shrubbery as a pool spread beneath them. Desperately, she beat Gelick's back. He knocked her aside, sending her rolling into a group of bramble bushes. Thorns tore into her skin as she scrambled to get up.

Gelick stood over Bry's motionless body. He changed back into his human form, but she could still see the blood on his face and hands. Staring at her brother, she looked for signs of breathing.

Gelick stumbled a few steps away from the body and smiled. "It had to be done," he explained. "Now, he can't poison your thoughts against me. He can't stop our love."

Adeline ignored his insane ranting. She went to her brother's side and laid a trembling hand on him. He didn't react to her touch. His chest no longer moved, not even to take a shallow breath. He was gone. She didn't realize when she'd began to cry, only that her cheeks felt wet and her vision had blurred.

Gelick took a step back in surprise and looked at her as if deciphering a puzzle. "I've freed you," he said. "This should be a joyous day. There is *nothing* to keep us apart now."

Unable to fathom his madness, she focused on clinging to the fabric of Bry's tunic as her body convulsed with sobs. He was more than her brother; they were best friends. He was the only one who understood, and even shared, her fascination with Earth.

She heard Gelick speak, but his words were drowned out by pealing thunder and heavy rain. When had it begun to storm? The sky was filled with clouds of the darkest gray. Static electricity snapped in the air. Suddenly, a bolt of lightning hit the ground by Gelick's feet. He looked at her in panic. It was his punishment, she realized. He'd broken one of their cardinal rules. He'd taken a life. His life energy was no longer in line with the energies of Calaspia. She almost laughed at the irony. Gelick was right. She was finally going to be free, just as he'd said, only it was at the cost of her brother. Where was the justice in this? There was no justice or good in the world. Faith was a joke, a lie she'd been taught to believe. She would put up with an eternity of his insanity to have Bry back. Nothing would ever be right again.

Gelick ran, but you couldn't run from something of this magnitude. A thick black fog surrounded him and she heard him scream with terror.

Her hair floated around her head. Her body felt heavy. The air felt heavy. She swayed from lightheadedness, sure she would fall over or throw up. Voices called out above the maelstrom. There were people approaching from the village, but she couldn't make out who they were. Her vision blurred and cleared again. The black clouds dissipated, and Gelick was gone.

With a faint smile, knowing he could never return to this world, she closed her eyes on Calaspia for the last time.

———

THE FIRST THING she was aware of was voices.

"It was the lake monster," a man's raspy voice said. Others groaned.

"Don't be ridiculous," another man snorted.

"The girl was found by the lake, soaking wet and covered in blood. What would you say was responsible?"

"Looks like some wild animal left those marks on her arm," a woman noted.

"And what would you call the lake monster? Tame?"

Everyone was quiet at that, until they heard her groan. She opened her eyes to a small room, dimly lit by candles and filled with people. They looked down on her with a mixture of concern and fear. "Can you tell us what happened, girl?" the first man asked anxiously.

"Seamus," the woman chastised, "you didn't even ask her name."

"Fine, fine," he relented. "What's your name?"

She opened her mouth to speak, but no words came out. What *was* her name? Why couldn't she remember? She sensed it, like a dream moments after waking, but she couldn't grasp it and keep it in her thoughts long enough to answer. "I don't know."

"Do you know how you were injured?" the woman asked softly.

Adeline looked down at her arm, blood soaking the simple cloth bandage. She could feel other bruises as well, but she had no memory of what had caused any of them. She shook her head and ignored the disappointment she sensed from those present. The men began arguing amongst themselves again at the probability of attack from sea creatures and other wild animals. The woman shooed them out of the room, sat down by her bed, and gently began brushing her hair. "It will be alright, my dear," she assured her. "You're safe, now."

A young boy rapped lightly on the door and stuck his head in the room. "Mother, I fixed the chain." At the woman's nod, he walked in and handed her a necklace. "I cleaned up the pendant some. There's a name on it."

"Thank you." She gave the boy a quick smile, and he left them alone, again. The boy's mother looked closely at the intricately engraved letters. "Adeline. Is that your name?"

She felt a knot of pressure in her chest, but words eluded her. Was that her name? The woman gently placed the necklace in her hand. "This is your necklace," she explained. "At least, we found it on you, but the chain was broken."

She stared at the letters carved in smooth metal. "Adeline," she said aloud, but felt nothing.

The woman patted her on the shoulder and resumed brushing her hair. "It will be alright, my dear. I'm sure it will all come back to you in time."

Maybe, she thought, looking down at her injuries. The real question, however, was did she *want* to remember?

———

TIME HAD NO MEANING. It swirled around him, pulling and pushing, corrupting his already shaky memories until he wasn't sure what was real and what was imagined. He remembered her face. That remained, even when he couldn't remember his own name. He didn't know who she was. Just a face. Her beautiful smile was enough to help him hold on when his body and spirit cried out for an end to this meaningless existence. How long before they stole that memory from him, too?

Shadows surrounded him. Howls permeated the darkness. He crawled through the sand, feeling his way by touch alone. A crack of lightning lit beastly forms a moment before they pounced. Claws ripped his flesh, just as they had a dozen times before. Every time was the same. His head swam with dizziness. His limbs felt weak. He couldn't survive too many more attacks. Somehow, they fed off his life energy. He wasn't sure how he knew what they were doing. The memory tied to the knowledge was gone. He watched them through the brief moments of bright light, punctuated with booming thunder. He could see his essence leaving his body, entering theirs, and strengthening the shadowy beasts. Closing his eyes, his mind wandered and floated along tendrils of energy. Just as he was about to give in and let them take him, his mind remembered something about energy transfer. *It could be reversed.*

His eyes snapped open and he pulled back from their attack. Energy began surging throughout his body. He pulled all the energy back and kept drinking all they had. His body glowed in the darkness. The beasts whimpered and retreated, visibly weakened. Gelick smiled. He was no longer the prey.

Stepping past the lifeless wisps on the ground, he

walked straight into a group of beasts to the left. They shuddered and skittered away. "Stop!" he commanded.

There was silence. The beasts bowed before him, their new master.

Thunder clapped the sky and the heavens unleashed a downpour of rain. The beasts shook and bolted for shelter. Lightning struck the ground a hundred feet away. A dark shape appeared in the sand. Gelick watched the figure, a man, as he scrambled shakily to his feet and attempted unsuccessfully to run through the sand. Fear and confusion emanated from the man in waves.

Ignoring the storm, Gelick walked toward the man. The air hummed with energy so thick, it was like walking through water. Waves of power pummeled him with each step. Lightning created a giant glass pillar beside him. Gelick paid no attention to any of it. The man ... drew him. He smelled of different energy. His life energy was strong. If not for the storm, the beasts would have pounced on this one immediately. It didn't really matter if he survived the weather; he was a dead man. All that was left to determine was the manner of his death.

"Help me! Help me!" the man screamed. "I need to go home. How do I *get* home?"

Gelick walked into a cloud of cool mist and saw the man slow down. Gelick continued his pace, but the man seemed oblivious to his approach. He stepped from the mist, and the man jumped when he saw Gelick appear suddenly beside him.

"Who are you? Can you help me? I need to go ..." were the last words he uttered before Gelick's brawny fingers wrapped around his neck.

Gelick pulled the man close and studied him. He

smelled of Calaspian energy, but there was something missing. "Who are you?"

The man's terrified gaze darted around in utter panic. "I ..." he croaked, his voice restricted by Gelick's hand clutching his throat. "I don't know." Tears streamed down his long frightened face.

"A fallen," Gelick reasoned. He wasn't sure how he could remember that, when he couldn't remember his own life in more than a few random snippets of detail, but he knew what this man was.

He sniffed again. The Calaspian scent, faint though it was, was intoxicating. Slowly, he drew on the energy. It was so much more satisfying than the dark energy he stole from the beasts. This was more than survival. It was about *thriving*. He felt energized and alive. He perceived memories of a world with expansive lakes and full lush forests. He saw her. That face. She was beautiful. What was her name? Frustrated, he fed on more of the man's energy. He paid no heed to the man's weak pleas for him to stop. He ignored the lighting glass towers springing up and the howling winds furiously whipping his clothes and hair. He discounted the feelings of speeding up and slowing down, of aging and growing younger. He wanted *that* memory. He wanted *that* name.

The man's body slumped. There was no more energy to take. He was gone. Gelick tossed the body to the side and howled into the maelstrom. It was such a powerful storm, so full of ... energy.

Gelick stood there, soaking up the power of the turbulent storm. This source didn't build memories, but it did leave him feeling stronger. Once the last of the winds had stilled, the beasts began to creep out slowly, watching him.

He pierced them with his penetrating gaze and spoke. "Find me more like him. Bring anyone lost in the desert to me."

As the beasts ran off to comply, he stared into the dark horizon. He would get his memories back. It was only a matter of time.

CHAPTER ONE

W arm sunlight shone through the leaves, leaving a speckled path on the forest floor. The wind blew fiercely, sending shadows scrambling in all directions. Using his stone hammer to drive in the last nail, Eric sighed with satisfaction. Finally, the work was done. He looked around, impressed with what he'd accomplished. It was a little further out from the main settlements than he would have preferred to build, but this place called to him, and he was taught to follow such feelings. Eric climbed the stairs and stepped out onto his balcony. Jumping onto a limb of a sturdy tree, he climbed up, higher and higher. Staring out at the vast horizon, over the sea, he knew this was where he must have his home. Now, he just needed someone to share it with.

"I thought I'd find you up here."

Eric looked up from his perch on the massive limb, a hundred feet above the ground. Just visible in the distance, a large hawk flew his way. With a seven-foot wingspan, the bird of prey deftly soared between the trees and came to rest on a nearby branch. A shiver ran along the hawk's animal's body, stirring feathers. A few seconds later, a man stood in his place. "Your parents are looking for you," he said.

Sighing, Eric stood and, with arms crossed, leaned forward, against a limb. Narrowing his gaze, he glared at his friend.

Narlic put up both hands and grinned. "Don't shoot the messenger. You know how your mom gets at Solstice."

"I know." He pushed off the branch, shifted into his hybrid hawk form, and squatted onto his perch. His elongated, scaled feet wrapped around the limb, holding him securely. Feathers covered his body in place of the clothes he'd worn a moment before. His hawk eyes observed with increased sharpness; they noticed movement and details in the surroundings undetectable by his human eyes. One taloned hand reached high to grip another branch. He flexed his wings as much as he could in the tree. "I don't see the point of sitting around all night waiting for something that probably isn't going to happen. I'd rather be out flying."

"And miss your mother's cooking?"

Eric grinned. It was true. His mother did make all her best dishes at Solstice. That alone was worth sitting around and listening to her talk of more grandchildren. The smile left his face. His mother was the real reason he dreaded this day. Every year, she got her hopes up, believing they would find a mate. Every year, she was disappointed.

"You never know," Narlic continued. "This could be *the* year."

"It could." But he wasn't holding his breath. It would happen when it happened. Without another word, he stood and stepped off the branch, letting himself fall until he was clear to fly. With wings spread wide, he glided in the direction of home. Narlic followed behind in full hawk form.

Gradually, Eric began to see a smattering of nests—homes—spread throughout the trees. Most nests were basic, with few comforts. Enclosed, they provided adequate protection from the elements, including the high winds at the top of the canopy, but the interiors were often much like a real bird's nest. Beds and floors were made of twigs and straw. Demonics, like him, usually preferred to revel in their animal forms; they were always present, part of them. Angelics, like Narlic, were either one or the other. In animal form, very little of their human sides were present; they sought out the same nests and perches as their demonic counterparts. Once they returned to their human forms, they sought the safety and ease of access of homes near the ground. The forest floor and first twenty feet above were littered with these small houses, complete with real beds, fireplaces, and stairs.

His parents' home was a mixture of these two designs. Outside, it looked like most of the other nest homes in the trees. High in the canopy, it had no access apart from flight. Inside was a different story. It was filled with furniture, books, and hand-painted family pictures. There was a loft on top, filled with straw and twigs. It was the perfect merging of the two styles, a compromise their father made to their mother, to ease her transition. She'd been a full human before their mating. This world had been an adjustment for her. But that was a long time ago.

The smell of freshly baked bread and cooked vegetables caught his attention. He inhaled deeply and let the delicious scents ease his mind. Angling into a swoop, he pulled in his wings and set down on the platform by their door. The moment it was open, the magnitude of his mother's feast hit him. There were food trays on every flat surface. Some were layered over other trays to provide space for even more food. There were sweets, breads, and savory dishes of every color and type. Appearing from behind the partition separating the front from a small kitchenette, his mother carried yet another tray.

Eric grabbed the tray and looked around for somewhere to set it down. "Are we feeding the entire kettle this year, Mother?"

She smiled prettily and brushed a stray hair from her face. "We can't have Solstice without a feast."

Narlic entered the home in human form and took an appreciative breath before heading over to taste a little something from every food tray. Eric's mom shooed him away with a delighted smile. For all intents and purposes, Narlic was an adopted member of the family. Their human tendencies and habits put him at ease, and Eric's mom loved having people around. Truth be known, he even looked like one of the family, with tan-colored hair and hazel eyes. His hawk form, a full transformation instead of a hybrid, was also of the same coloring, indicative of the red-tailed hawk, whose spirit they all shared. Narlic inclined his head apologetically and started organizing the trays, but the moment her back was turned, he went back to sampling food.

"Sure, but you never make this much food," Eric went on. "I don't think even Narlic, Ephraim, and I can eat all this." While it was true they could eat a lot, this much food would last them for months, even when distributed to his other four siblings and their families.

"We need enough for your mates and their families," she said matter-of-factly before heading back to the kitchen.

Eric rolled his eyes and set the tray on top of two other dishes. "Mom ..."

"Don't 'Mom' me. This is *the* year." She rinsed off a dirty pan and set it on a towel to dry, then moved on to the next one that needed cleaning.

"And what makes you think this year will be any different from the past three hundred?" Grabbing a towel, Eric started drying cleaned dishes and helping her put them away.

She stopped for a moment and looked at him. Her eyes glowed. "I can feel it. It's going to happen today. And you feel it, too." She poked him in the chest. "That's why you've been working so hard on your house. You finished it, didn't you?"

"Today," he reluctantly admitted, "but that doesn't mean anything. I've been working on it a long time. I had to finish eventually. The timing is just a coincidence."

His mother simply smiled and returned to rinsing dishes.

Eric felt a shiver run down his back. His gaze sharpened, but the room felt odd—real, yet not. He almost missed the dish his mother handed him. "Besides, it's not up to us," he said at last, shaking off the strange feeling. "It will happen when it's meant to happen. Where are Ephraim and Dad?"

"Your father is getting more pumpkin seeds for my muffins. As for Ephraim, I saw him fly west a while ago. I hope he returns soon. It isn't good to be too far out on Solstice."

"I'll go find him," Eric promised and set down the towel. He needed some air, anyway. A flight would do him good. Besides, he had a feeling he knew where to find his energetic younger brother.

———

ERIC FLEW low to avoid the strong crosswinds near the caves. Sure enough, he could hear his brother inside, yelling with excitement. The caves were a popular spot for young hawks; they tested their skills and courage by dropping into the caves from above, circling down, and flying back out the opening. It sounded easy. It was anything *but* easy. The caves were narrow, so there wasn't a lot of room for larger wingspans to spread. This meant that only younger, less experienced fliers could attempt it. Add to that the strong wind currents that swirled within and around the caves, and you had a very dangerous place to fly. But that didn't stop headstrong hawks like his brother who were drawn to the danger, excitement, and magnetic fields produced by the minerals in the cave rocks.

Walking carefully up to the opening, Eric looked in and called out to his brother. Most of his words were drowned out by the loud winds, but Ephraim felt his presence and looked up. "Come on in," he said aloud and telepathically.

Eric shook his head and motioned for Ephraim to come out. Circling around, he soared from the roof of the cave, landing gracefully next to Eric. "What's up?"

"Mom wants us both home. Solstice is about to start."

Ephraim nodded. "Alright, after this last jump."

Before Eric could stop him, Ephraim took a step back and fell into the cave again. He shook his head. Standing and waiting, he watched his brother circle a few times, fly up, and swoop to circle some more. "Come on," he prodded telepathically.

Ephraim gazed up and sighed, nodding. Circling for momentum, he started his ascent. His form was perfect. Suddenly, a gust of wind caught him off guard, knocking Ephraim into the side wall. His wing crumpled from the impact, and he fell, hitting several jutting rocks on the way down to the bottom of the cave. Eric watched helplessly as blood began to pool on the cave floor around his body and head. "Ephraim!" he yelled.

His brother moaned and shifted, but his eyes remained closed.

Anxious, Eric's eyes darted around. There was no way down to the cave floor and back except through flight, and his wingspan was too wide for the cave. He could get help, but Ephraim might not have that long. He had to get him out and take him to a healer immediately. Eyeing the dimensions of the cave, he thought he might manage it, *if* he got enough momentum to fly up before he pulled in his wings. It was a long shot, but he had to try. If he didn't, his brother could die. Taking a deep breath, he prepared to jump in, but pulsing energy shot through him, staggering him and leaving him dizzy. He looked around in confusion. His surroundings were strange, the colors different than they'd been a moment before. He peered at his arms and hands. His skin tingled and glowed. Turning in the direction of the village center, he saw the entire area covered with a similar glow. Solstice.

"No, no, no," he repeated. He was caught in Solstice. Those selected for Solstice found themselves pulled from the regular time phase until they'd found their mate and completed the joining. Then, they phased back into time with everyone else. He'd heard it described many times from many people over his lifetime. Some found that a single hour out of phase was only moments in regular time. Others found time passed slower here.

Every mated pair phased at a different interval or speed. And the only person he would be able to interact with until he came back would be his mate. He looked back into the cave and saw a shimmering outline of his brother's life energy. With a tremendous amount of effort, he stepped back. He couldn't help him until this was done. He just prayed his phase was faster than regular time. If he was lucky, he could return with little time actually having passed here. Either way, he had no choice. He would find his mate, complete the joining, and come back to save his brother. No problem.

Taking another deep breath, he put a hand to his chest and felt the pulse of his energy. Once his breathing was in sync with that energy, he felt it shoot forth and travel outward ... to the area of the last Earth portal. Eric groaned. This had just gotten a lot more complicated.

CHAPTER TWO

"**B**reathe in. Breathe out. Good, you're doing much better." The young doctor smiled amiably and, looking at her file, provided instructions.

Nancy sat back and took a couple more deep breaths. It was amazing how much easier it was to breathe here. There was very little pain in her chest. After listening to the instructions, she gathered her bag of medicines and prescriptions, ready to head home.

"How did it go?" Paul asked. He stood and followed her from the waiting room, out to his car. He offered her an umbrella, but she walked into the rain. After countless days of rainstorms, she was used to them.

"Good. They say the treatments are working. The doctor told me to keep taking my medicine and gave me prescriptions to take back home, in case I have any flare ups once I leave."

Paul cranked the car and began driving back to the airport. "I don't know. You might have to move down here, like Mom."

Paul's mom was Nancy's Great-aunt Phoebe. Like

Nancy, she suffered from breathing problems. When Phoebe's parents moved up northwest for her father's work, Nancy's grandmother was okay, but Phoebe became very sick. Eventually, she returned to Louisiana, and her breathing problems improved. Doctors could never figure it out. Nancy's grandmother never had the same problems and married out west, so she'd never moved back, but they had kept in touch; the two branches of the family were still fairly close.

It was Paul who'd suggested Nancy come visit after he heard of her bouts of an incurable respiratory illness. He'd finally convinced her to do so after getting his mom's doctor to call her doctor and arrange a consultation. The trip proved great and relaxing. She'd felt better than she had in years, but it was time to go home. Nancy hugged her cousin at the terminal gate and boarded the plane. She was asleep within minutes.

In her dreams, she was falling. Air rushed past her body. It should have terrified her, but it felt strangely comforting, like the wind was embracing her. Her sandy, long hair whipped around her face. She took control of the fall and glided over snow-covered mountains and through mammoth clouds. Massive lakes and serpentine rivers stretched out below. Animals skittered through treetops and along the ground far below. Her eyes could make out incredible details from a good distance away. She could almost guess where the animals would travel. Closing her eyes, she trusted in her body to do what it needed to. She gave in to the freedom.

Suddenly, Nancy felt everything change. She opened her eyes to darkness and found water surrounding her body, pressing in, filling her lungs. It was freezing cold. She gasped for air, but there was none. She couldn't breathe and began to flail and struggle until there was no energy or oxygen left in her body. A dazzling light shone deep in the water—the light of magic and freedom. All she had to do was swim to it.

Why was she so afraid? Just swim! She could do this. It was simple. The water was restorative, a blessing; it was good and necessary. But her body wouldn't listen. It was afraid and resisted. She couldn't swim, it reminded her—she would drown, become lost in the depths of darkness, never to be found. But if she didn't try, she would drown anyway. Nancy's body and mind battled for supremacy. Fear held her back. The darkness closed in around, smothering the light until it was only a pinprick. She stared at the dot of light, holding on to it, a small glimmer of hope, until it disappeared.

"We are about to make our final descent. Please, buckle your seat belts and prepare for landing."

Nancy blinked and opened her eyes. She was on the plane. Groggily, she made sure her belt was buckled. The dream had felt so real. She could still remember the feeling of her lungs burning with pain. Her skin tingled and blood pounded in her chest and limbs, and pulsated within her head.

"I love your eyes. Are they contacts?" a young flight attendant asked as they passed each other in the aisle.

"Oh, no, they're natural," she answered automatically. People were always commenting on her icy-blue eyes. Everyone in her family had blue eyes, but hers were just a little different, lighter, with a magical sparkle. Normally, she made polite conversation, giving thanks and smiling; today, she was in no mood to chat. She walked on before the woman could say anything else.

As she made her way off the plane, she felt her chest

tighten even more. Her body was weak, tired and heavy, just like she'd felt before her trip. Nothing had changed. Home, sweet home she thought with a cynical smile.

Strolling through the airport, Nancy looked longingly at the planes taking off. How she wanted to turn around and get on one of them and go somewhere else—to freedom. She thought of the first part of her dream, where she'd soared through the clouds. Truth be told, she hated heights; she'd despise being that high up, but the thought of freedom to go where she wanted and no longer be tethered to the ground was seductive. She could leave today, start a new life. She felt "almost normal" in Louisiana. She could go there ... or somewhere else. There *had* to be other places where she could live without this constant pain.

Her feet faltered turning toward the ticket counter. Her body was ready to go. Her mind had to be the responsible one and remind her not to jump into any hasty decisions. If she wanted to move, fine. She could do research, travel around, find a place she liked, and move—with boxes, fresh clothes, and a plan, like any normal person.

"Take a leap of faith," her heart yelled. A tear slipped down her cheek.

The air buzzed with energy. Why did this moment in time suddenly seem so very important? Without question, something big was coming. The pain in her chest increased and crushed all thoughts. She'd figure this out later. Right now, she needed to brave this breathing attack. Her mind wouldn't be able to focus until it was over.

Hailing a cab, Nancy hurried to her small mid-town apartment. Immediately, she turned on the humidifier and water fountains in every room. She popped prescription pills and downed a glass of tepid water. The water helped. The pills ... not so much.

Feeling trapped and helpless, she fell onto the couch and tried to concentrate on breathing techniques. While they helped to a degree, she still gasped for air. A bath always helped. Scrambling into the stiflingly small bathroom, she pulled off her clothes and turned on the water. After dumping half a bottle of cucumber-scented bubble bath into the tiny tub, she turned on classical music and slipped into the welcome sudsy warmth.

Scented bubbles floated on top, gathering along her hips and legs. A large bath ball fizzed loudly upon hitting the water. Soothing fragrances filled the air.

It did little, however, to relieve the tightness and pain in her chest. This was more than the usual breathing problems. She was experiencing a panic attack. What if she *did* have to move? What if she moved and it *didn't* help? Yes, it had helped her great-aunt, but they were different. The doctors couldn't even figure out what was wrong with her. They treated her symptoms with a lot of trial and error, and fair amount of guesswork. What if these breathing problems worsened? *You couldn't live if you couldn't breathe!*

Inhaling slowly and focusing on the scents and music, her heart continued to beat too quickly. She could feel the heavy pulses through her palms, which lay on her thighs. Closing her eyes, she leaned her head back against the beige fiberglass tub wall and felt tears of frustration well in her eyes. Why couldn't she just get better? She was tired of being sick.

Nancy took a deep breath and tried to contain the panic. Things weren't over yet. Sinking further down, Nancy practiced breathing techniques until the frantic beating of her heart slowed and the pain subsided. Slowly, her breaths became deeper and longer. Her pulse slowed. Tight muscles relaxed. The pain subsided. She remained in the tub until the water grew tepid. Then, waiting for the tub to drain, she stood and toweled off, dressing quickly.

Now that her breathing was under control, she was starving, but she was in no mood to cook. Her sister, Cindy, wouldn't be home from work for a few hours. If she wanted to eat before morning, she'd have to go out now, alone. Slipping on a light sweater and an old, worn-out pair of sneakers, she headed out.

Where to go? She wasn't really in the mood for anything in particular. She just wanted to eat *something*. As she drove past several fast food places, restaurants, and all-night convenience stores, she spaced out and suddenly found herself on the outskirts of the city, with nothing for miles in either direction. To make matters worse, the low-fuel light was blinking, and she had no idea how long it had been on. She pulled onto the shoulder of the road and turned back, but she didn't get far before the car died, out of fuel.

"No, no, no, no, no." She slapped the steering wheel and tried to get the car moving. It was no good. Gazing around, she saw distant city lights. The road, however, was dark and void of traffic.

Reaching into her purse, she pulled out her cell phone and called her sister. The screen lit up for a second before the low battery indicator blinked and the phone chimed as it turned off. The screen was dark. With the breathing issues and panic attack, she'd forgotten to charge it when she got home. Now, the phone was dead and she was stuck at the side of the road, in the middle of nowhere.

When Nancy opened the car door, a cold blast of wind hit her hard and she quickly closed it. She'd forgotten how cold it could get here at night. Honestly, she'd forgotten it was winter. The weather had been so warm and pleasant on the trip, she'd spent most of the time wearing shorts and sandals. There were one or two times a light sweater had been required, but the next day it had proven warm again. Even the nights hadn't gotten this cold. Given the freezing temperature, there was no way she could walk back to town. She was stuck. Feeling helpless and frustrated, she rested her head on bent arms against the steering wheel and cried.

Sometime later, she noticed light moving across the interior of the car and looked at the road, hoping to see a passing vehicle. What she saw instantly suppressed the depression.

The entire night sky blazed with spiraling, colorful streaks of light. They moved and danced like the Northern Lights, but this wasn't the Arctic. She stepped outside and noticed it was no longer cold, but refreshing. A warm misty rain started to fall and the sky grew brighter. The top of her head and everything down to her toes tingled. A healing warmth from the light permeated her body and she felt light, as if floating on air. Her skin shimmered. In fact, everything seemed to shimmer. The trees and road looked different. They seemed ... magical.

Lightheaded, she got back in her car and leaned against the headrest. The lights in the sky dimmed, but everything still had that shimmering glow. All of a sudden, brilliant light burst from the sky and penetrated her chest. It felt solid, like a rope tethering her to something. Countless emotions and thoughts flooded her mind, then quickly faded, but the feeling of being connected to *something* persisted.

———

GELICK AWAKENED upon experiencing a sudden surge of energy. Quickly running to the window, he saw light shoot from Calaspia to Earth. He grinned. This meant a Calaspian would be traveling between the worlds, and a human of great power would be vulnerable.

"Find the Calaspian mate," he ordered the beasts.

The wispy phantoms hesitated. They preferred lost and abandoned souls who sometimes appeared in the sands, but they knew better than to disobey his order. As one, they raced off.

He paced excitedly around the small, broken abode. Holes in knotted walls allowed in ample sunlight. The door was merely a crevice in the rocks, just wide enough to squeeze through. Even the window was a hole, but wider than the others. The place was falling apart, but it was enough shelter to protect from the fierce desert sun. He wasn't worried. When it came to unexpected storms, he purposely went out to soak up their energy.

It had been ages since anyone had breached the barrier. It would be nice to get his hands on one of them again, and a newly transformed Calaspian mate would be a rare treat. Their life energy was always potent and fresh. It had been too long since he'd been able to siphon any real energy from anyone. Apart from random thoughts and unconnected images, memories were growing increasingly hazy. Now, there were blank spots—half memories like faded dreams— in his recent memory as well. If not for the ability to modify time fields and siphon energy... he'd become like all the other Calaspian outcasts.

Gelick walked over to his latest victim, a hapless soul, barely even human anymore, and prepared to seize his remaining energy. The man, chained to a wall, didn't look up. Gelick drew the man's energy inward and felt recharged. With the barest of sighs, the man expired. Reaching out with his mind, Gelick modified the time field around him, speeding it so the man's body turned into dust.

He sighed, already hungering for his next meal. Mortals always seemed to find themselves lost in time—they were easy to come by. But they died too quickly if he simply drained their energy to be a fully satisfying meal. Sometimes, he could keep them going a little longer, like he had this one, taking a little at a time and allowing the victim to recharge—a trick he'd figured out after years of practice.

At one time, he'd enjoyed the occasional Calaspian; they left themselves vulnerable when traveling between worlds. Unlike humans, Calaspians could go on indefinitely, at least until they lost hope and became a fallen. Even then, he enjoyed spending a long time with them. The beasts were fools not to go after them more often. The rewards were worth the dangers. As immortals, they were teeming with energy, a buffet of life force. But the beasts never went after full Calaspians unless they were injured in some way. They were too afraid to take the risk. Not Gelick.

Occasionally, he glimpsed his victims' memories in the transfer. It helped fill in some gaps in his own mind. He was banished. That is what they termed him. They hated him. Even the defiant ones feared him. Those glimpses of a connection to something he could *almost* remember were seductive, and as motivating as the energy his meals provided. But the travel between worlds stopped, and full Calaspians no longer appeared outside of their home realm, so he had to make do with what the time beasts could find him: mortals and fallen Calaspians.

Fallen retained a spark of immortality, though the well had limits. And they were far more likely to end up lost in the gap between time and space. For a long time now, preying off the energy of fallen Calaspians was how Gelick managed to stay strong and retain whatever memories he had. He didn't gain new memories. Fallen were much like him in that respect. They forgot their pasts, but their spirits remembered, and that energy was delicious.

The phantoms purposely chose easy, frail targets who provided very little life energy to drain. This was why the phantoms were so weak and easy to control. He went after bigger score and took the prize. Drawn to his strength and power, they hunted for him, bringing him many more victims than he could find on his own. When first he was banished from Calaspia, the beasts hunted him. Now, he ruled them. And when pickings were slim, he fed off of them.

Gelick reached his mind out to them. He sensed from their excitement that they were in pursuit. Good. It wouldn't be long now.

CHAPTER THREE

Once she felt steadier, Nancy exited the car again and walked to the side of the road. Squatting, she studied the grass and flowers, touching them. The flowers were large with vibrant, fluorescent swirls of oranges and yellows. They emitted a sweet calming fragrance, vanilla mixed with lavender.

Her gaze drifted to gravel tucked in the grass, and she picked up several pebbles. Even they seemed to have changed. Their marks and imperfections were beautiful, like an oil painting. Her skin pulsed where she held them. She could feel energy and life develop around her.

Giddy, Nancy danced across the road. The air was remarkably rich and clean. Gazing around, she tried to take it all in. Where to focus? What to do? She ran her hands through her loose hair and laughed.

That feeling of being connected to something persisted and she felt an overwhelming urge to go to the city. Something important was waiting there. She took a step in that direction and stopped. A wailing howl pervaded the silence of the night ... and she felt something else. An intense sense of danger.

Looking anxiously around, she warily returned to her car and locked the door. Three dark, shadowy creatures ambled from nearby bushes and approached slowly. Canine in appearance, they were tall and lithe, with shadows dancing around their bodies. Their eyes glowed like candle flames as they watched her.

The creatures drew closer. She watched, staying as still as she could, hoping they'd not notice her, but realizing all too well that they knew she was there. She felt somewhat safe in her car, until one of the shadow creatures poked its ugly, ghostly head through the passenger door and snarled. Its teeth were stark-white, long and sharp.

Eyes wide with fear, she shrieked and, forgetting she'd locked the door, scrambled to open it. After struggling with the button, she managed to open the door ... to another snarling beast. Quickly pushing past, she ran full-speed down the road. Hearing their feet hit the ground behind, she ran even faster. They were snapping her heels, but she didn't dare look back.

She ran to a building. Pulling open the door, she scrambled inside and slammed it behind. It took a minute for her breathing to slow enough for her to hear. She saw a small sitting room, a long kitchen and rear door. Hastening forward, she discovered stairs behind the door leading to a second floor. Peering hard, she sighed with relief—there was nothing outside. That relief, however, was short-lived. A board creaked and she heard a low rumbling growl. Without moving, she glanced at the reflection in the nearby window and saw a shadow creature coming down the stairs. This time it looked more feline, with long sinewy back legs and a long thin back. Wrapping her hand around a vase on a table by the door, she flung it at the beast and raced outside.

For what felt like hours, she ran through back yards, streets, into and out of homes and businesses. Every time she thought she was safe, another creature found her. Some were already in the buildings. Others followed her inside by drifting through walls. There were cats and canines, as well as large beasts; one even resembled a bear. Given the abundance of buildings and streets, she knew she'd made her way back into the heart of the city—but *where*? Everything looked different. Just like the flowers and rocks by the street, everything had changed. Some buildings were ornate and beautiful with scrolling borders and thick flowery vines covering walls and roofs. Being inside them made her feel strangely happy and energized ... at least until the beasts found her. Other buildings, however, looked broken and ... sick. They made her feel bad just to be near them.

Confused, and tired of running, she headed down yet another street and stopped. Six beasts stood in her way. She backed up and heard a familiar growl. A quick glance behind confirmed three more creatures were there. Though surrounded, calmness washed over her. "Yeah, though I walk through the valley of the shadow of death," she quoted quietly, "I will fear no evil." Though unsure why the Bible verse had popped into her head at that moment, she was grateful for the comfort it gave. Strangely, she wasn't afraid. No fear clouded thoughts or senses.

The sound of rushing water drew her attention and she turned to a building made of heavy stone with sparkling gems speckling the walls. A waterfall surged over the threshold while bright pink and purple flowers grew from a sea of green vines and bushes clustered around the building. Trees were covered in bright blue green leaves. One of the beasts suddenly lunged forward, startling her; she darted toward the building, sprinting through the waterfall.

Beneath the flowing water, time froze and a feeling of peace prompted tears, before she burst through to the other side. She waited for a moment, expecting the beasts to jump through the water or enter via the walls. None came. She waited a little longer. Her breathing slowed. There were no growls, no creaking boards. Walking slowly, she cautiously explored the room.

The building was equally amazing inside. Walls were made of dense stone and thick wood, like trees growing out of a boulder or mountain peak. The gemstones outside were also in here. A huge crystal chandelier bathed the room in bright light that reached the farthest corners. Every stain-glassed window was a jewel-encrusted masterpiece. Stunned, she realized this was her church.

Her eyes widened, and exploration grew more exciting. This was definitely her church. Where normally there were simple wooden pews, there were large moss-covered logs. Underneath them and the altar, the floor was covered in grass. The walkways were comprised of smooth cobble-stones. A giant oak tree took up the back corner of the church. One of its massive roots rose from the ground and curved to form the altar; upon it sat a simple wooden chal-ice. A tree limb—supporting a brightly lit lantern—trailed the back wall, seemingly molded into the stone.

Another tree twisted around to form a circular staircase to the balcony, which was woven of branches and leaves. Nancy walked to the top and, sitting on the surprisingly comfortable balcony, peered outside. The world seemed dark in comparison to the dazzling beauty inside. She could view many blocks in all directions. Beyond the property line of the church, shadowy beasts paced. They did not come closer than the street. Most of those who'd pursued her earlier seemed to have lost interest and left, but a few remained.

Feeling safe, she rested amid the leaves and fell asleep.

———

ERIC FELL TO THE GROUND. His head still spun from the journey through the portal. He studied his surroundings. The ground was uneven, rocks and roots breaking up small patches of grass. Bright red and blue flowers bloomed all around, even on the sides of trees, whose trunks hummed with energy and life. Fluorescent moss clung to everything.

So, this was Earth, or at least a time-shift version. His heart beat wildly with excitement. He was the first Calaspian to set foot here in a very long time. This extraordinary moment would be retold to his people for generations; he was now part of living history. Part of him wanted to explore this world, to see everything the time shift would reveal to him that no other Calaspian would see, save for those who might one day mate with a human, but there was no time. His mate was alone and afraid, and his brother could be dying. Sightseeing would wait.

He inhaled deeply, then exhaled, expanding his senses until he found her. Relief washed over him. For the moment, she wasn't afraid. The intensity of her feelings before had nearly driven him mad as he'd crossed through the portal. This wasn't unexpected. He knew this shift out of time must be confusing her; it was strange, even to him. It had to be unnerving for someone unaware of what was happening or why. But the fear he'd felt was more than that. Something was *wrong*. She was in danger, and he had to get to her quickly. His protective instincts were in full force.

She was his mate. He had to find her. She needed him as he needed her. He wanted nothing more than to take flight and get to her now, but the portal had dropped him amid a grove of thick trees. There was no room to spread his wings, so he'd have to walk a considerable distance to be clear of them.

It didn't take Eric long to realize what had caused his mate so much fear. The beasts stalked quietly for a good two hundred feet before coming into sight one by one. He felt their presence as he tracked them with all his senses. He'd heard stories of these phantoms who preyed on those adrift in the seas of time. They usually weren't a problem in Calaspia, even at Solstice. Strong wards, as well as the power Calaspians possessed, kept them away. As with most predators, they looked for easy prey, but these seemed different somehow. They weren't afraid of him. Instead, they appeared to be leading him into some kind of trap or ambush. He sensed more of them up ahead. They would attack once their numbers were great enough to ensure success; he needed to be airborne before then.

Seeing his moment, he grabbed a low-hanging branch, pulling away from their hideous snarling mouths. A couple raced forward and tried to climb it. They were unable to get very high, but the tree did shake from the fierce attempt. Others began to ram the tree, trying to knock it down or him off. Scrambling to a higher limb, Eric jumped to another tree. And so he continued, climbing, jumping, and scrambling, until he was finally high enough to spread his wings and take flight. From the sky, he watched the beasts converge. Their raucous howls filled the night. If the beasts were out in such large numbers, he had even less time to find his mate and return to Calaspia. Neither of them would be safe here.

He flew with all his strength for the better part of a day. Finally sensing her presence, Eric slowed and tried to pinpoint her exact location. His mind wandered, imagining what she'd look like. Would she be fair-skinned and meek or fiery and strong? Would she have light hair or dark? Blue eyes or brown? Had she already discovered her hawk nature?

His train of thought stopped abruptly. What would she think of him, with his hawk wings and features? Would they intrigue or frighten her? He imagined her eyes filled with fear and repulsion, and felt uncertainty course through his body. That wasn't how he wanted their first meeting to go. Of course, he'd have to show her his form and reveal everything, but he must go about this carefully. He had absolutely no idea how she'd react. The last thing he wanted was to cause more fear. She'd likely respond better if he took his human form for the initial interaction. That in mind, Eric set down and shed his hawk form. When he heard the growl behind him, Eric wondered if this had been the best decision after all.

———

THE MOSS-COVERED floor was unexpectedly comfortable to sleep on; the cool, damp moss cushioned nicely. Nancy rolled over and stretched, feeling more rested and energized than she had in years. Beautiful rays of faint colored light from the moon shown through the window, casting an enchanting spell over the room. It was still dark outside. Whatever this place was, regular rules of day and night didn't seem to apply. It was peaceful and quiet. She could stay here forever.

Awareness tugged within, breaking the spell. There was

pressure in her chest, but not the kind she normally experienced before a breathing attack. This felt like she was being pulled or compelled toward something. Once again, she sensed being connected to an entity outside herself. Only this time, it seemed closer. After running for so long, she'd nearly forgotten that feeling. Sitting up, she looked out the window and scanned the streets. She wasn't alone. There was a shadow of a man passing between the buildings a couple blocks away. Leaning closer, she strained to see him better, but he disappeared around a corner. She kept looking to see if he'd re-emerge.

Who could he be? During all her running, she'd seen no signs of other human life. What if he was stranded like her? He could be hurt or need help. Or maybe he knew where "here" was and how they could get home. She looked around the church balcony wistfully, remembering her thoughts moments earlier. What if there was a way home? Did she really want to go? Then again, could she live *here* forever? At some point, she would have to eat something, though she had yet to feel any hunger since the shift to this strange reality. Logic dictated this could not last if she were, in fact, still alive, not that she was even sure of this fact. Perhaps this was all some weird afterlife world and there was no going home. But if she were still alive, and she did have to eat, she'd have to travel outside the church to find something ... and face those beasts again. Yes, if he knew a way home, she needed to find out. Either way, she had to learn whatever he knew.

The man darted from between the buildings that had been blocking her view, with phantom beasts chasing him at full speed. He ran and jumped, ducking this way and that to evade their claws and teeth. Remembering her own desperate run, she felt her heart stop. She had to help him get to the church grounds, where he'd be safe. Running down the stairs three at a time, she nearly tripped on the bottom step, but she didn't let that slow her. Spinning to avoid a fall, she kept moving and dashed out and across the lawn. One of the beasts had overtaken the man, pinning him to the ground. Without a second thought, she left the safety of the churchyard and rammed her shoulder into the phantom's body, knocking it off the man. Both she and the beast tumbled. Her head hit the hard ground.

Momentarily dazed, she saw the man standing protectively between her and two beasts. Somehow, the church was behind her again. She wasn't entirely sure how that had happened. Three more beasts approached, and one charged the man. Her mind cleared instantly and she saw what she must do. As the man readied to take a hit, she jumped up and grabbed his arms, pulling him back. The look of surprise and shock on his face as he fell back, onto to the grass, would have been comical if she hadn't been knocked down by the same rampaging beast. Thinking it would rip her apart or tear into her flesh with its immense teeth, she was shocked when all it did was loom over her. She pushed against it, but found her arms lacking strength. Her entire body felt weak and useless. Her head swam with dizzying lightheadedness. What was it planning to do to her? This was worse than what she'd expected. How could it steal her strength? She couldn't fight or do anything but lie there and pray for this to end.

———

ERIC LOOKED up from the ground in confusion. What had happened? Why had she knocked him over like that? The phantom beasts surrounded his mate's limp body and howled with excitement over their victory. His head spun around, but the beasts seemed to be ignoring him completely. Seeing the holy building behind him, he realized why. This was protected ground. They could not cross here. That was why she pulled him back, to protect him.

Heart surging with pride, love, and an intense desire to save his mate, Eric shifted into his stronger hybrid form and flew toward the cluster of beasts, grabbing them one at a time whenever he flew up to cast them aside. After a couple of passes, the weaker phantoms ran off, afraid of his might. That left the one beast actively feeding from her energy. Emboldened by its surge of strength from her, it was not about to let Eric take its prize without a fight. Growling, it broke off contact and turned to stare him down.

Eric dove downwards, trying to get a grip on its body so he could lift it up like the others, but it snapped at him with each try. Committing himself to a final attack dive, he flew into the beast and transported it with him down the street. The phantom bit his shoulder and clawed at his arms and wings as it began to drain his life energy. Accepting the pain and embracing the dizziness the phantom's attack caused, Eric flew as far as he dared and dropped the beast. Weak from pain and blood loss, and energy low, he returned to recover his mate's body and take her to the holy ground where they'd both be safe.

He tried to make it all the way to the building, but his free wing would not oblige. Unable to carry their combined weight any longer, they tilted and spiraled erratically. Finally, his wing gave out completely, and he fell in a controlled roll, wrapping them protectively with his good wing, and spinning so he took the brunt of the fall. He landed hard on his bad wing, injuring it further. Barely conscious, he forced himself to shift back into his human form.

His mate groaned in his arms and began to rouse now that the phantom was no longer stealing her energy. He felt her slender body shake when she struggled to pull him up. Gathering what little strength was left, Eric staggered into the building with Nancy's assistance, through a misty doorway of falling water. Once inside, he collapsed onto the soft grass floor. Her body falling beside him was the last thing he sensed before falling into a deep healing sleep.

CHAPTER FOUR

Nancy pushed up from the ground and tried to figure out what had happened. The last she remembered, the beast was on her. Then, she was back on the grass, with the stranger beside. She felt weak. What had the creature done to her? She couldn't see any visible injuries. Was it some kind of energy vampire? Whatever it had done, the effects seemed temporary because her energy was returning ... slowly. Things could have gone a lot worse.

She eyed the large, unconscious man. He must have run them off and pulled her back to the safety of the church grounds. From the look of his injuries—bright red gashes—it wasn't without a cost. Some were still bleeding. Pulling off her sweater, she ripped off the sleeves. After wetting the fabric at the waterfall, she quickly returned and began wiping blood from his cuts. Some were deep. She wiped gently but firmly, removing all traces of dirt and grime.

Removing more strips from the now ruined sweater, she tied a makeshift bandage around the more severe cuts on his shoulder. It pained her to think of him enduring these injuries for her. She could almost feel those claws ripping through her own shoulder—so much so, she rubbed her shoulder for several seconds to lessen the phantom pain. Why had those beasts done this to him and not to her? She'd gladly have taken his place, something she'd actually considered when she'd raced over to lead him to the protected church grounds ... but *he'd* saved her. She owed him her life. That hideous beast would have kept feeding off her if he'd not intervened.

She checked his injuries twice more, bandaging and cleaning where necessary. Collecting the dirty fabric, she took it to the waterfall and rinsed it, setting it aside in the event it might be needed again. Her mind wandered. Who was he? How had he come to be here? He'd helped her when he could have stayed where he was and remained safe. That spoke well to his character.

Nancy brushed hair from his face and studied his handsome features, peaceful in sleep. She stared at his captivating face for several minutes. The many lines around his lips and eyes suggested a person who frequently smiled and laughed. His body possessed the lean muscles of someone who acquired strength through physical activity instead of a gym—and primarily outdoors, given the deep tan.

She touched his chest and felt energy surge between them. It pulled, expanded, and drew her closer. Her eyes watered as an abundance of emotions washed over her and she kissed the stranger softly on the lips. The man moved and murmured in his sleep. The kiss deepened and the energy encased them. Forget wanting to stay on that balcony alone. She wanted to live in this moment *forever*, lost in a kiss, here with this man!

With great effort, she pulled back, ending the kiss. Nancy's head swam with dizziness. What was that? And why did she feel so close to this stranger? Tenderness filled her heart and hesitantly, she touched his chest again; the energy burst did not recur. Then again, maybe it had never left. Goosebumps covered her flesh. Heart pounding, she looked at him with bewilderment.

"Who are you?" she wondered aloud. And if he kissed like that while unconscious, how much more gratifying would it be to kiss him while he was awake? No. She shook her head. She needed to keep such thoughts from her mind. He was a stranger and she didn't go around kissing strangers, no matter how amazing they looked. And she certainly didn't go around kissing unconscious men. What was wrong with her? She *could* wake him up, so she could kiss him properly. No. She shook her head again. Couldn't she go ten seconds without thinking about kissing this man? Taking a long steadying breath, she closed her eyes for several seconds, then opened them again to observe him. ... Apparently not.

Nancy sighed and stood, walking across the room to put some distance between them. Now that the distraction of caring for his wounds was over, and she was starting to regain control over her inhibitions, fatigue was returning. She felt drained and more than a little confused. Nothing about this day made sense. That feeling of being connected to something was stronger than ever, and it centered on this man. Somehow, she felt joined to him.

The pounding of rain on the church roof echoed through the room. Her lips curled up—how she loved the rain. It always made her feel recharged and alive. Perhaps it could erase the effects of whatever those phantoms had done to her and help her gain some clarity over this situation. Recalling the courtyard at the back of the church, she made her way down familiar yet different corridors. Veins of glowing stone ran along the wooden walls. The same glowing stones made up the floor, lighting the way until she reached the end of the path. Passing through the iron gates, unchained in either world, she slipped off her shoes and stepped onto the cobblestone path.

The courtyard was just as she remembered it, only more. Filled with colorful flowers and lush moss, she stepped into the rain and peered up, letting water wash over her. Her dizziness disappeared in an instant. Above, the vast sky was dark and peppered with bright stars of every color. Rain, warm and comforting, seeped into her clothes and soaked her hair. It was like being tucked in a thick warm blanket on a nippy winter night. She pressed her toes into the cool, wet stone floor, enjoying the sensation. Eyes closed and head upturned, Nancy was unwilling to move from her spot.

She felt his presence before she heard his steps. Her pulse quickened, and she opened her eyes. Feeling strangely nervous, she turned and watched him approach from the shadows. A breath caught in her throat. His deep golden hazel eyes burned as they gazed at her. He stepped into the rain, and she saw her makeshift bandages grow transparent from the moisture. "You shouldn't get those wet," she stated, taking his arm to lead him back to the cover of the pathway. "Sorry about that. I'll re-bandage them with some dry cloth. There are still pieces of my sweater inside."

"It's fine," he smiled, amusement in his voice and eyes. "I'm a quick healer, but we can go back inside if you like." She looked wistfully back over her shoulder at the court-yard. "Unless you prefer the rain," he added, seeing her reaction.

"Huh? I, yeah, I love the rain. It hardly ever rains here. Well, not 'here' I mean. At least not *this* here, wherever here is, but the real here, the normal here. I'm Nancy, by the way." She extended a hand in greeting.

The man grinned and took it lovingly in both of his. "I'm Eric."

Her heart sped up and her skin flushed. "Eric," she repeated softly and swallowed hard, allowing him to keep her hand. "Um, well, we should be safe here, I think. So far none of those creatures has tried to enter the church grounds."

He nodded. "It's a sanctuary, a holy place of power and faith. My home has a similar ward around it."

"Where are you from?" Curiosity cut through the unexplained nervousness she felt with him in such close proximity. But the desire to kiss him was no less intense with him awake.

"It's complicated." His eyes lost their humor and gained a touch of fear and uncertainty.

Nancy raised an eyebrow. "I've spent the past ... who knows how long ... 'cause the sun never rises here. But it feels like one or two days have passed, running from phantom creatures that can pass through walls. Nothing looks right. We're in a place that was a normal building, however many days ago it was, and is now some kind of weird stone building, with trees running through it and a waterfall door. I think I can handle 'complicated'. Whatever you have to say, I'm just relieved to be talking to another living human being."

"I'm not human," he admitted wryly.

Her eyes narrowed, and she scanned him from top to bottom. "You look pretty human to me."

Taking a deep breath, Eric gazed deeply into her eyes, and changed. Feathers suddenly covered his body. Mammoth wings sprang from his back. His feet bore talons, and his deep golden-red eyes lost their human appearance to take on that of a bird. Shocked, Nancy jumped back, pulling her hand from the fingers that now sported claws. The pulsing muscles around his strange eyes made his face appear pained. It was quickly gone, however, as though he were trying to hide his disappointment by her reaction.

She felt a mixture of confusion and guilt. It made no sense. Why would he care what she thought of him? Why should she feel guilt at disappointing this stranger? She didn't know him. She didn't even know what he was or why he was here. And she certainly didn't know why she couldn't stop thinking about kissing him. If anything, this new appearance heightened her desire, and while it was unexpected, she couldn't help thinking how incredible he appeared. But it was more than just his exotic good looks that captivated her—she felt drawn to the person inside, the soul she innately knew hadn't changed with the transformation. One to trust her instincts, she instantly knew this was a good man. If only his eyes didn't look so strange.

"Okay," she said, finding her voice at last. "So, not human. What ... *are* you?"

He stared for a moment, gauging her reaction. When he spoke, his eyes never left hers. "I'm a Calaspian ... more specifically, a demonic." She glanced at the angels fighting demons on the stained-glass windows of the main building. "That's not what we are," he clarified, "although it was where my kind got our names. On Calaspia, there are demonics and angelics. For thousands of years we traveled freely between our world and this one. Because of our appearances and abilities, we were often mistaken for the same beings who became our namesakes."

"So, you're some kind of alien?"

"Alien?" he repeated the unfamiliar word.

"From outer space, another planet." She motioned the sky.

He nodded his understanding. "It's more of another dimension connected by the seas of time."

"Okay," she said uncertainly. Her lips opened and closed several times before she blurted out, "Can you do something about those eyes? I cannot for the life of me tell where you're looking, and I'm not going to lie ... they are *totally* freaking me out."

———

ERIC LAUGHED WITH RELIEF, catching her off guard. He felt her confusion. She thought her words would upset him, but instead he felt excited. She could have asked him to change back to human form. Instead, she only asked he change his eyes. That was very encouraging. More than willing to accommodate such a simple request, he closed his eyes and willed them back. Opening them, he was rewarded with a relieved sigh and nervous smile. Her shoulders relaxed and her body seemed more at ease. He motioned a bench under the walkway and waited for her to sit. Joining her, he allowed enough space to avoid making her uncomfortable.

"The story of my people began an unknown time ago. There was a man of great faith and poor luck. All manner of hardships plagued his life. Everywhere he turned, he saw only suffering. Yet, he didn't falter. He believed things would always work out for the best, given enough time. He traveled to a land of suffering and dedicated himself to easing the pain of others. There, he met a woman with skill in animal magic. She could adopt the form and traits of animals to help in times of great need. Together, the pair continued his work, bringing comfort to those without."

Eric paused to watch her reaction. She was listening, but seemed detached. She was difficult to read. He couldn't be sure if she believed him. "Yet again, bad fortune followed the man," he continued. "His wife was injured while defending an innocent. As he held her hand and watched her life force wane, the man gave thanks for the time they'd had. Although his heart broke, he didn't lose sight of his belief that all things happened for a reason."

Nancy's spectacular ice-blue eyes blinked. Through their shared connection, he could sense her sadness for the man's pain and suffering. The depth of her empathy surprised him. "Then, on the eve of Winter Solstice, at the moment of greatest darkness, he found his light. Her heart stopped beating at the exact time between the twodays and great magic was released with her passing. The spirits of all the animals she'd ever called materialized and bound themselves to receptive humans across the realm. One of those spirits took refuge in her, and through its power, she was healed."

Nancy's lips parted and she released the breath she'd been holding. Eric felt sorrow lift from his chest. "Those who now held animal spirits flocked to the couple, and he told their story. His faith spread. Others began to believe. One by one, they learned of a new ability to move between realms. Only those with unwavering faith could navigate the currents. Those who gave in to fear and began to doubt the inherent goodness of life, found themselves lost, cast to other worlds. They were called fallen. Those who were fallen forgot all that they were and became one with their new worlds. Those with strong faith discovered a land nestled in the sea of time. They called their new home

Calaspia and settled in the sanctuary. And so they remained."

"You mean they hid."

His forehead furrowed in confusion. "What do you mean?"

"I mean, it must be easy to stay optimistic and faithful if you hide in some sanctuary with a bunch of other people who believe like you do. That first guy, he immersed himself in the suffering of others, trying to help people, and still stayed positive. He didn't hide from life and all its unfair suckiness. I can't imagine he'd be happy in this paradise world, when he knew that in the other worlds, people were dying and being tortured."

He felt a well of emotions bubbling inside her.

She closed her eyes and shook her head. The emotions dissipated. "I'm sorry. I have no idea why I got carried away like that. It was wrong of me to say those things. I don't know you or your people. I have no right to judge anything on a two-minute conversation."

Eric paused. He'd expected questions and a good bit of doubt and fear, but he hadn't expected a philosophical discussion. What would it be like to live in a world of death and pain? His mom rarely talked about her childhood on Earth, but he knew it hadn't been easy. He tried to see things from her perspective. If he'd lived through immense suffering, would his faith be so strong?

"I can't say you're entirely wrong," he allowed. "Our founder and his wife didn't stay in Calaspia. You're correct about that. They were there for its founding, but never stayed long and, as far as anyone knows, are still out there traveling between worlds, helping others. Perhaps the rest of us took the easy path, but it wasn't always that way, and there were reasons for the choices my kind made. Many did seek refuge and safety. I suppose they saw Calaspia as their reward for a lifetime of suffering. I can't speak to individual motivations. Many of our elders eventually follow the example of our founders. They say it's a calling, a desire to leave our world and return to where they're needed. There were others who saw Calaspia merely as a safe resting place between journeys. For a while, many continued to travel between the worlds, even Earth. It was those interactions that provided names to describe the two branches of our kinds—"

"Angelics and demonics?" she interjected.

"Yes," he smiled. "You see, while we're animal and human hybrids, angelics retain more human nature and often assume full animal forms or full human forms, as the situation dictates. Demonics are prone to take hybrid forms like this," he indicated himself, "mixing and fully integrating our human and animal natures. Although we can take full animal forms, it's more difficult to do, and isn't the form we prefer. Because our animal spirit is more prevalent, we tend to rely heavily on instincts and can become agitated easily. That's also why your people likened us to demons. Fear of our visits grew. Some of our kind were killed, not just here, but on other worlds. The angelics had the benefit of their easy-to-maintain human forms and temperament to help them blend in, but eventually they were hunted as witches and forced to return to Calaspia. The connection between our worlds grew thin and became difficult to travel. Some were lost trying to return here or go back. And so, we've maintained our distance."

"Then, why are you here? Or why am I here? And where exactly is *here*?" she asked curiously.

He smiled understandingly, and his hand reached out instinctively to touch hers. Her skin felt soft under his rough fingertips, and a breath caught in his chest. She reacted similarly, but didn't flinch or move away. Her face softened as she smiled; it was beautiful. She accepted his touch. Eric looked into her eyes and felt a shock course through his body when pretty, sparkling eyes stared back. He felt her goodness, her spirit and soul, just as he felt their connection, clear and undeniable. Desire built and threatened to overwhelm his senses. He wanted to hold her close, kiss those soft, inviting lips, and stare into those beautiful, magical eyes for all of time. "You have the most beautiful eyes I've ever seen," he whispered, wonderstruck.

Her mouth parted in surprise. "You like my eyes?" Her voice was barely audible.

"Very much." He touched her face and she leaned close. "I have no idea what I was saying," he admitted.

Nancy laughed. "Uh ... about where we are, I think."

"Right." He dropped his hand. Inhaling slowly and deeply to steady his thoughts and emotions, he continued. "We're here because of the Winter Solstice. Every year, on this day, we have feasts and celebrations."

"Because that was when the first guy's wife was saved and all of your kind was created?"

He smiled. "Yes, exactly. We use magic and rituals to form connections through the plane of time. No one knows exactly how it works, but any unbound adult can be affected. We shift out of phase until we find the other person *in* phase with us, and pass through the temple archway together."

"This is the plane of time?"

"It is."

"Are we still on Earth?"

He nodded.

"Then why can't I see anyone else? And why does everything look so different?"

"We can't see anyone else, and they can't see us, because we aren't moving at the same speed as they are. Only you and I are in sync. Things look strange, because everything is more a spiritual representation of itself. We're seeing things as they truly are. Places with dark energy will be ugly and murky. Places like this church, holy places that may appear normal in a regular time phase, show their beauty."

They gazed around the courtyard and took in the peaceful serenity. The rain had slowed to a fine mist. Moonlight shimmered on puddles and glowing flowers.

She moved closer to him. "I've always felt at peace here, even when everything looked normal. I think that's why I found my way here when I was running. I didn't know where I was going, yet somehow I ended up here."

His fingers tightened slightly around hers. He ached to embrace her. "We often sense things we cannot see. Places like this leave their impression on us."

"And you were brought here because of some magic rituals?" she asked softly, gazing at him.

"We *both* were." His voice was equally soft.

They stared at each other, feeling the pull of their mutual attraction, even if Nancy didn't understand why.

"Why me? I'm not one of your people. Why did I get sucked into this Solstice ritual time-shift thing?"

Eric paused, unsure how to answer. From what his mother had told him, although some human marriages were arranged for political or monetary gain, the majority of humans were highly protective of their freedom to marry a person of their choosing. They didn't welcome outside forces or persons making the choice for them. Calaspians were staunchly independent, as well. They'd broken away from all they'd known to create a new society in a new world, after all. But they'd done so with unwavering faith in a greater power providing guidance toward the best possible outcome. That faith, and centuries of experience, taught them to accept divine mating without question.

"You're afraid again," she said matter-of-factly. "What are you afraid to tell me?"

Through their connection, she could perceive his emotions as easily as he could hers, so he shouldn't have been shocked. "When we phase out," he explained, "the person we're in sync with is our divine match. To leave this place, this time, we must *both* accept the mating, the joining, without reservation. Traditionally, that has meant a complete connecting of body and soul."

Her eyes widened. "I'm not one of your people," she said again. "Why am I here?"

"In the past, when the connection between our worlds was stronger, matings between our kinds were not unknown to occur. My mother was from Earth. In these cases, the human gains our animal spirit and our immortality."

She shivered.

He ached to hold her, comfort and kiss her. "Ever since I saw light travel to Earth, I've been in unfamiliar territory, as I know you have. Even though it happened to my parents, I never once imagined it could happen to me because that was so very long ago ... one of the last times before travel became restricted."

Shocked, her eyes widened with trepidation. She was quiet for several moments as hundreds of thoughts flit through her mind. She closed her eyes, took a deep breath, and then stared intently. "You're saying you and I are some kind of ... soulmates?"

He nodded once.

"Why should I believe any of this?"

He understood and respected her skepticism, but there was one thing she wouldn't be able to deny, at least to herself. Slowly, he leaned close, an inch from her ear.

Her breathing quickened as she watched him through partially closed eyes.

"Those who are mated feel an overwhelming attraction to one another. The urge to join is strong, nearly uncontrollable." His hand brushed her arm, and their mind connection flared.

Her thoughts flashed to memories of a stolen kiss while he slept.

Eric grinned. He had thought it was real, but he hadn't been sure until just now. Their connection was already exceptionally strong.

She closed her eyes and swallowed heavily. Her entire body shook, though he could sense she fought to control it. He experienced the same and he ached to hold her. Their proximity was both sweet and intoxicating ... and an exciting yet frustrating exercise in discipline and restraint.

After a long moment, Nancy reluctantly pulled away and stood, putting distance between them. She ran a heavy hand across her forehead and then clasped her hair when her body refused to cease shaking.

He half expected her to jump into his arms and give in to the passion he knew she felt. She took another step back, into the misty rain.

Breathing slowly, the rain washing gently over her, she met his gaze. Her body was once again under control. "I don't know what you're expecting, but it's not like I'm going to sleep with you just because you say we're supposed to. I mean, as pick-up lines go, it's original, but as far as I know, you could be full of crap." Nancy's sparkling eyes stared defiantly, reading him and analyzing the situation.

Eric smiled. Her will was strong, and her intellect was sharp. "I expect nothing. I have no idea how this day will go." He laughed softly thinking, not for the first time, how much he wished he'd asked his father more about the day his parents had met.

As he looked around the room, he thought of his mother—calming his harried thoughts for the first time since arriving here. Many of these windows and statues reminded him of her and the few precious possessions she'd brought to Calaspia. He walked over to a stained-glass window depicting an image of a family huddled together beneath a star. "My mother told me many times how her people believed mating ... er, marriage is a holy union meant to bring two people closer to God. A ... sacrament ... she called it. She says the imperfect love of mates, er ... spouses," he corrected himself again, "is a reminder of God's *perfect* love for us all. It's a conduit through which God delivers wisdom, comfort, and other graces." He turned back to Nancy. "I don't consider mating to be simply an excuse to indulge in physical desires or a means of procreation. I know it means much more than any of that. Besides, being together physically isn't enough; our minds and souls must also accept the mating. Most are required to stand upon the temple grounds in Calaspia and announce their intentions to accept the mating before Solstice magic returns them to regular time, but every mating is different. The magic is ... unpredictable."

"So, not only do you want me to sleep with you, you want me to commit my entire life to a stranger based on your word that we're meant to be together? Oh, and I'm supposed to travel to a world in another dimension and no longer be human for eternity?"

Frustrated, Eric raked a hand through his hair. How had his father explained this to his mother? How difficult had it been for her to accept what he'd told her? He thought of all the little things his father did to make her feel comfortable in Calaspia. He'd never really appreciated how much their mother gave up, what a leap of faith she must have made to accept the mating and accompany their father. "I'd never presume to force you into anything. The mating must be voluntary to be successful. If you come with me to the temple in Calaspia," he shut his eyes and took a deep breath, hating to say the next words, but knowing they were necessary, "you may renounce the mating if that's your choice. Apart from accepting the mating, it's the only way to return to our own phase and lives. Either way, we need to return to Calaspia. The journey will take some time, so you can consider all I've told you, and we can become better acquainted. No decision need be made until we reach the temple grounds."

She imagined renouncing the mating and felt a sharp prick in her chest. If she did this, there was no going back. She'd never see him again and never know what they could be together. What if he was right, and they were destined for each other? They'd be joined for life, an *immortal* life. No matter what she decided, she was making a decision that would irrevocably change both their lives. How was that fair to Eric? As far as she could tell, this was all on her. He was completely committed to accepting the mate Fate chose for him. He was committed to her. She felt her breath catch. She needed time to think, time to get to know him, and time to decide which crazy decision to make. "How would we get there?" she asked hesitantly.

"Technically, we could will ourselves there right now, but that's difficult without practice, which I don't have. If you're afraid or unsure of your destination, you could drift somewhere else and potentially become a fallen. Thankfully, portals exist that make travel between our worlds easier. There is one about a day's travel from here, or at least what would be a day if time were moving."

"You said people were getting lost just before everyone stopped coming here. Was that through the portals?"

He nodded reluctantly. "It's happened. That's why it's important to enter these portals with as little fear as possible."

"Okay, so we just have to travel a day with those creatures out there to get to a portal that could erase my memory and send me to some random world. No big deal. There's no reason to be afraid." She laughed nervously.

Eric moved toward her, and clasped her arm. His wings flexed open slightly. "I'll protect you," he vowed.

Her gaze softened as she eyed the injury on his wing. She reached out, then pulled her hand back. "Does it hurt?"

"Only when I fly, which means, unfortunately, that we'll have to walk during most of the journey, until it heals. But I won't let them harm you."

"I'm not sure what scares me more, traveling on the ground with those gruesome beasts or the thought of flying to stay clear of them. I'm not exactly a fan of heights. They kind of terrify me. So, I'm not sure if I even want to ask this, but why not wait until the wing heals and then leave?"

Eric closed his eyes. "Just before we shifted, my brother was flying around in a deep underground cavern. The winds in there are strong." He swallowed heavily. "Some headstrong fliers like to test their wings there." He felt emotion leave his face and voice as he continued. "My brother was caught in a current and propelled into the side of a cave wall. He fell just before I phased out. No one else knew he was there, and I won't know how much time is passing there until I get back. When you go out of phase, sometimes you move at a speed faster than regular time. Others phase out at a slower speed. Our time here could be a minute, or a few hours, there. If I don't get back soon, he could die."

"I thought you were immortal?"

"We don't die of old age or get sick. We heal quickly when injured, but we can be hurt," he motioned his own injuries, "and we *can* die."

She eyed at his wing with understanding and determination. "Then, what are we waiting for? You should have said something sooner. There'll be plenty of time to talk while we walk." She slipped on her shoes without untying them and moved at a brisk pace through the church.

Eric's eyes widened in amazement. Her resolve was clear. He could still sense her fear, but she wasn't letting it control her actions. She'd face unknown dangers and travel to a world she didn't know with a relative stranger, all to save a man she'd never met and had no reason to believe even existed. He knew, in that moment, he'd truly love this woman for the rest of his existence. Reverting to human form, he joined her by the waterfall door. She was letting the water flow over her shoulders and back.

Calmed, as she was by the rain in the courtyard, her eyes felt as if they were glowing when she regarded him quizzically. "You didn't have to do that," she said. "Change forms, I mean. Not on my account. Didn't you say ... demonics prefer their hybrid forms?"

"Generally, yes, but everyone has their own comfort level with each form, based on how often we take them. My family has spent enough time in human form to feel at ease. At least until my wing is healed, I thought it might make you more comfortable if I took this form."

"That's very considerate, but I'm okay. Your other form doesn't make me uncomfortable. Take whichever form you like. It's going to be a long trip." She licked her dry lips, and he heard her thoughts add, "Wow, he really does look damn sexy either way."

Her cheeks reddened and he wondered how embarrassed she'd be if she knew he'd heard her. Unable to help himself, he placed a hand on her back and whispered in her ear, "I'm glad you approve of my appearance."

Her breath caught. "How?"

Telepathically, he responded. "Be mindful of your thoughts, or you could accidentally send out ones you don't wish to be heard. It's one of our gifts."

"So which way is that portal?" she asked awkwardly.

CHAPTER FIVE

Nancy felt herself quiver with embarrassment. He could hear her thoughts. Could he hear what she was thinking right now? What else had he heard? Then again, he didn't have to tell her anything. He could have kept it a secret, and he hadn't. Instead, he'd given her that warning. He smiled, clearly amused. Okay, she couldn't fault him there. She'd be pretty amused by what he'd heard, too. But, thankfully, he wasn't trying to make her feel bad about it.

Letting it drop, he pointed to the east and with a hand still on her back, led her gently in that direction.

Nancy didn't see any beasts lingering around the church grounds, but faint howls could be heard in the distance. "Do we have a plan for getting past the beasts, or are we hoping to get lucky?" she asked, walking at a steady, slightly slow and nervous pace.

Eric stopped and stared into her eyes. Her mixed emotions calmed and tense muscles relaxed. It was almost the same feeling she had when standing in the rain, only this feeling was coming from him. He was calming her with a simple look. But how?

"They're attracted to fear," he answered softly.

She leveled a look. "Seriously?"

He nodded.

"And the more of those that get attracted to you, the more fear you feel, and so more come, and so it goes on?"

"Basically, yes."

"Okay, so I get why they were chasing me, but why were they going after *you*? I thought your people had too much faith to be afraid."

"If there was no struggle between faith and fear, faith would be meaningless," he postulated. "Besides, I was worried about you," he confessed, his expression earnest. His hands cupped hers.

She felt that now familiar pull between them. An invisible energy pulsed, joining them in inexplicable ways. "What will I say?" his voice echoed in her head. "Will she believe me? What if she rejects the bond? Am I ready to be a mate? So much fear. She's in danger. What if I can't protect her? I'm unworthy of such a miraculous gift. Please let me be worthy of my mate. Please let her remain unharmed."

Nancy felt her throat constrict with emotion. Whether he was aware of the words she'd heard in her mind, she couldn't say, but she discerned the sincerity and knew, without a doubt, that every one of those thoughts had run through his mind before he'd found her.

Eric continued speaking aloud, softly and sincerely. "At first, I was nervous of how our meeting would go. I ran through the different ways I could explain things to you, and considered all the ways it might go badly. What if you didn't believe me? What if I frightened you? Then, I felt the danger you were in and found the phantoms on this side of the portal. After that, I stopped thinking of anything but finding you before they could do you harm."

She felt warmed by the admission. Before they'd even met, he was searching for her, worried about her. She'd thought she was alone, that no one knew where she was or that she was in danger, but *he* knew and had come for her. He protected her. "And now?"

"Now, I worry about keeping you safe and saving my brother."

A picture of an injured man flashed through her mind. She wasn't sure if it was her imagination or a real memory, and it was too quick to get much more than a general impression, but Eric seemed unaware she'd seen anything.

"But I'm not afraid. I've found you, and that gives me hope. *You* give me hope."

Turning back to the path, they began walking again. Eric's hand returned to her back. She wondered if she should object to the contact, but truth be told, she was comforted by it. The last time she'd been out on these streets, she'd been alone. Having someone with her was a definite improvement. It made her feel ... safer. As they crossed the border of the church grounds, her steps faltered. She turned her head side to side, anxiously scanning the streets for danger.

His hand stroked her back reassuringly and he held her hand with his free one. He helped Nancy step over a gnarled tree root growing through the street. She allowed him to lift her over a larger root that followed. He did it with such ease, his hands feeling natural around her waist. Gently, he lowered her, their bodies nearly touching. Her pulse quickened.

"If you believe everything always works out for the best,

what's there to worry about?" Her voice was slightly breathless, but she didn't care. He already knew he affected her, and true to his word, he hadn't forced so much as a kiss. He was a perfect gentleman. She felt safe with Eric and for reasons she couldn't understand, she trusted him completely. He was a stranger and yet, she felt like she was walking with a long lost friend.

"Just because things work out for the best doesn't mean there's never pain or suffering. It means, when times are hard, you don't lose faith. You know there's a reason, and things will get better. And," he added with an impish grin, "I *am* half human. My siblings and I inherited much of our mother's willful independence."

She smiled in return, glad he was shaking off his earlier worries. "You say that like it's a bad thing."

"Not bad," he corrected. "Sometimes we're just a little too headstrong for our own good. We make things harder than they have to be."

"Doesn't everyone?" she quipped. Nancy kicked at a stray pine cone and sighed. The rain picked up again, drenching her clothes and hair. She faced the sky and closed her eyes. "I love how much it rains here. Does it rain like this in Cala ... Calap ... Calac-uh."

"Calaspia," he said slowly.

"Calaspia," she repeated, looking at him, their faces nearly touching. "Does it rain there?"

"It rains. Not quite this much, but it rains."

Water streamed down his face. She looked down at the useless bandage remnants, now barely covering the cuts. He'd received these injuries because of her. "How long will it take you to heal?" She fingered the unblemished skin around the cuts and felt her skin tingle, like a static shock, but more subtle. Eric didn't seem to notice.

He glanced at the shoulder and shrugged. "A few hours or so, maybe longer for the deeper gashes."

"And the wing?"

"The same. I may be able to fly sooner if need be, at least for short bursts, but I'd like to give it as long as possible. If I push it before it's ready, it could end up giving out when we most need it." Taking her hand in his, they continued walking.

"What are those creatures, anyway?" she asked. Even while considering unrelated topics to discuss, she found herself thinking how pleasurable his fingers entwined in hers felt. "They all look so different," she continued. "Some were like hounds and some looked like big cats. I swear a few even resembled bears and alligators."

"They were once Calaspians."

She looked over in surprise, but waited for him to explain.

"I've told you how Calaspians become fallen when they lose faith."

She nodded.

"When Calaspians becomes fallen, they usually retain a spark of their divine gifts. They always have the potential to return, should they work through whatever crisis of faith led to their fall. It rarely happens, but the potential is there. Most of them simply acclimate to their new world and live out their lives, unaware of where they'd come from. This isn't the case with banished.

"Occasionally one of our kind, with leanings toward violence or selfishness, starts causing grievous harm to others, which is a betrayal of our entire world. It causes the divine spark to become weak and corrupted. The darkness within results in a Calaspian being forcibly ejected from Calaspia. Unlike fallen, they can never return. Their divine spark extinguishes, leaving an emptiness within. Most fade and cease to exist. We can't live without that light, that connection to the divine. Some figure out a way to survive by stealing what they need. They're naturally drawn to that spark of divinity in others, and because of their selfish natures, they learn to grasp onto that life force and pull it into themselves. It fills a void within, but the effects are temporary, and they need to continue to prey on anyone who possesses that spark. It makes them feel closer to what they were. And, to feel that closeness, they'll hurt whoever they need to.

"Most fade, becoming shadows of their former selves, driven by instinct to survive, but eventually unable to shift forms or remember former lives. They float through the seas of time and continue to prey on anyone lost traveling between the worlds, but they typically search for weak, easy prey. I've never heard of them being this aggressive in the past. Then again, once we stopped moving between realms, we stopped encountering them. Much could have changed since then. Perhaps they've grown desperate from lack of victims."

Nancy thought of how sad it all was. Every phantom was once a person with hopes and dreams. But they hurt people, she reminded herself. Everything that happened to them, they brought on themselves. It was still tragic, but her sympathy for them only extended so far.

They stepped into a sizable forest at the edge of town. Large gnarly trees twisted up high, into a canopy of sparkling leaves. Flowers of every color and shape spiraled around the trunks and covered the mossy ground. Nancy looked around in amazement that they'd made it this far without encountering one single phantom. Had she really been that much more afraid before? She glanced at her hand tucked in Eric's and realized he was a big part of the reason she felt so at ease. Regardless whether everything he'd said was true, she couldn't deny that being with him affected her.

"My sister will never believe any of this." Nancy laughed to herself. She herself hardly believed it.

"You have a sister?"

"Cindy. She's younger than me. She's a vet ... a doctor for animals," she clarified. "She's really good with them, and with patching me up when I have one of my klutzy moments and injure myself in some bizarre 'Nancy' way," she said, adding air quotes. "She jokes I have the grace of a fish out of water. Cindy actually taught me most of the fantastic field medic skills I used on that." She motioned the bandages. "I was a terrible student ... or she was a terrible teacher. Maybe both," she grinned.

"I wouldn't say that. I'm a hawk in a kettle full of adventurous thrill seekers with more guts than sense half the time. I've had my share of bad patch jobs. You did fine."

She smiled humbly. "What about your brother? What's he like?"

Eric smiled, but she could see the concern on his face. "Headstrong, stubborn, and usually the cause for emergency healing needs."

"Is he younger than you?"

Eric nodded.

"Thought so. Must be a younger sibling thing."

They laughed knowingly.

"Maybe so. Ephraim and I have four other brothers between us. I'm the oldest. He's the youngest. The rest mated years ago. They calmed down after they started their families, but even before their matings, I don't remember any of them being as rambunctious as Ephraim. He's a bit of a daredevil. And he's fast, one of the fastest fliers I know." His face beamed with pride. "He'd do anything for anyone. He once took the blame for the roof of a meeting hall being destroyed when his friend fell through it while trying to do some complicated spinning flight maneuver. Ephraim had to repair the roof and clean the hall every week for a year after that. Of course we all knew what he'd done, and everyone, family and friends, took turns sneaking in to help when the elders weren't around."

"That sounds like fun. I guess you come from a pretty close-knit group. Are there a lot of you?"

"Hawks, angelics and demonics combined, we have a couple dozen family groupings, but the avian species are relatively close. We tend to nest in the same forests, and we share a council of elders."

"Wow, and I thought *we* came from different worlds. I don't even know most the people in my own apartment building. I did get my neighbor's mail once by accident and took it over, but she wasn't home, so I left it by the door."

"Well," he pushed a low hanging branch out of the way and helped her through the opening, "my world is your world now. If you want it."

She faltered. "And my world?"

"I look forward to seeing it with you."

"And what if I wanted to stay in my world?" Hadn't she just this day wanted to leave her home and travel somewhere new? But a new world? That wasn't quite what she had in mind. She was too chicken to board a plane to another state, and now she was going to travel to another *dimension*?

Eric stopped and grasped her other hand. "If it is indeed my destiny to live in this world, I'll do so willingly, by your side."

"You'd leave your world for me?" she asked, shocked. How could he be so willing to change his entire life, leave all his family and friends, for a stranger?

"Am I not asking you to consider the very same thing?" he asked, his expression solemn.

"But you don't even know me."

"I know you're my mate."

"Do you? What if you're wrong? What if this is all some big accident and we're not destined for each other?" He had to see this was crazy.

"And which do you hope for?"

She shook her head, confused. "What do you mean?"

"Do you hope I'm wrong, and this is all a mistake?" he asked gravely. "Or do you fear it's a mistake and hope it's real?"

She had no idea how to answer. Which *did* she hope for? Which did she believe? Everything he said felt true. This *felt* real. She couldn't deny they shared a connection, but what if he was wrong about what it meant? Could the Solstice magic be wrong? He should at least know what he was committing to, before he threw away an immortal life on some stranger. "You don't know anything about me," she argued. "I'm a terrible person to sleep next to. Just ask my sister. She still complains of all the bruised ribs I used to give kicking her while we slept when we were kids. I eat salad with my fingers, I can't stand when corn gets mixed in with potatoes, and I can't eat a peanut-butter sandwich unless it's open-faced, preferably with the crust removed and a heart drawn in the peanut butter." She paused upon seeing the huge grin on his face. "What?"

"You keep focusing on the idea that I might find being with you unpleasant, but I haven't heard you express any concerns you might have or find being with me. Aren't you worried about my bad eating and sleeping habits?" Before she could , he pressed a finger to her lips. She half closed her eyes at the feel of his touch. "Just think about it." Turning, he returned to leading them through the trees.

She could swear he'd adopted a smug-like swagger in his step. Not that she could blame him. He was right. She hadn't considered she might not want to be with him. It seemed obvious. Of course, he'd have bad habits and would annoy her, but none of that was important. She still wanted to be with him. What was the matter with her?

"Has anyone ever rejected a mating?" she asked before she lost courage.

Eric slowed, and all signs of humor left his face. "Twice. A lion angelic and a wolf demonic, both to human mates."

"What happened to them? Did they marry other people?"

Eric stopped and faced her. He spoke softly. "In the case of the lion, his mate was already betrothed to a human nobleman before they met. She feared what would happen to her family if she backed out of the marriage. Ultimately, she chose to sacrifice for her family instead of following her heart. The Calaspian understood the pain of that difficult decision as only a mate could. He didn't try to stop her. Once the mating was renounced, their bond was never completely severed, for they still loved each other. He felt her pain, her joy, and her suffering until, at last, he felt her death. After that, he retreated into a life of solitude, away from our people's villages."

Nancy's heart melted with sadness at such a tragedy. Then, she realized, that could be Eric. She held the power to sentence him to the same fate. He stood on the precipice between love, family, and a future, or loneliness and eternal sorrow. And over what? She wasn't trying to save her family or make some grand sacrifice. Eric would be completely justified to hate her indecision, and yet she sensed none of that from him. He was nothing but patient and kind with her. "What about the wolf demonic?"

Eric looked away. "Her story is ... unpleasant."

"And the last one wasn't? What happened?"

He looked at her for a moment and inhaled at length. "This happened a long time ago, before I was born, but according to the story, the wolf demonic was young, naive, and inexperienced. When Solstice magic brought her to her mate, she quickly succumbed to feelings of passion, giving herself wholly to her Earthly mate. After the physical joining was complete, she revealed who and what she was. He called her a witch, an evil spirit set to seduce him and rob him of his soul. She cited their attraction and mental connection to support her claims, but he used those same things as evidence of her using black magic to cast a spell. His harsh, open rejection blasted her back to Calaspia and severed their connection, save for the child they'd conceived ... Once she learned of the pregnancy, it crushed what was left of her. She descended into madness and became fallen, living out the rest of her life on the world that had destroyed her."

Nancy's mouth dropped in shock and a tear rolled down her cheek. She shut her eyes, letting waves of empathy wash over her for the ill-fated people she'd never met. Taking a steadying breath, she smiled sadly.

"Are you okay?" Eric regarded her intently.

"Yeah, just thinking. You know, life really sucks a lot of the time. When one of my kind has leanings toward violence or selfishness and starts causing grievous harm to others, they aren't cast from my world. We have to live with them and all the pain they cause. But even without that, there are people whose lives are terrible and never get better. They suffer unbearable tragedy, lose their families or homes, live with constant physical and emotional pain, never achieve dreams, or just never get delivered from whatever struggles they have. You said, 'When times are hard, you don't lose faith. You know there is a reason, and things will get better,' but even in a paradise world like the one you come from, for some people, life doesn't get better. And if some people have lives like that, then *anyone* could. We aren't guaranteed a good life, that things will always work out, that our dreams will come true, or illnesses will end. Sometimes they do. Sometimes they don't."

Nancy spun and stared at the trees, deep in thought. "Most of the time it isn't even the big things that bring us to our knees. It's the day-to-day events, a constant stream of stupid, small, annoying, meaningless things that never seem to end or give relief. It's struggling year after year to get ahead, only to find yourself standing still, always getting what you need to survive, but never anything more. Even with absolute, unwavering faith and acceptance that things happen for a reason, that there's some meaning to it all, life can still really suck." She turned back. "How do you hope for and believe in a bright, happy future, when you have faith and accept that sometimes that isn't what's for the best?"

Stunned, Eric could only stare.

With a soft sigh, Nancy ran a hand through her hair. "Sorry, I'm not usually so philosophical, at least not out loud."

"But it's something you think about."

"Sometimes. I used to have this concrete belief that things worked out and got better, that dreams could come true. I was optimistic. But then I look around and see examples where that doesn't happen, and everyone just settles and accepts the lot they're given and stop trying to achieve anything better. They do responsible things and get knocked down again and again. They say be happy with what you've got, and I totally get the idea of focusing on gratitude and accepting struggle and hardships. I see the connections sometimes, when others are lamenting the unfairness of life and how horrible an event or something was, and I see where it led to something good. But ironically, the stronger my faith in the meaning of it all, the less sense everything else makes, the less I know what I *should* be thinking, or feeling ... or doing right here and now. How do you completely immerse yourself in a goal when you've already accepted that you may not achieve it, and that's okay? How do you know what dreams to have faith in and to fight for?"

"I don't know. I guess ... when the motivation is right, when you're being led where you're meant to go ... you just know. You feel it. Maybe you were right," he acknowledged. "Maybe we Calaspians have isolated ourselves instead of facing real challenges to our faith for too long."

"Or maybe just long enough." She felt knowledge and clarity stir. "Maybe ... maybe the isolation served some purpose, but that purpose has ended now?" She shuddered, the feeling of clarity gone, a hazy imprint on her mind and thoughts.

"What do you mean?"

Nancy blinked and shook her head. "I ... I don't know. I don't know why I said that." Confused and mentally drained, she laughed nervously. "So, do you have any hobbies?" she asked, needing to change the subject.

CHAPTER SIX

"Hobbies?" He arched an eyebrow and eyed her quizzically. "I don't know what that is."

"Hobbies are things you do for fun, in your free time, you know, when you aren't traveling across dimensions rescuing people."

She grinned, and he grinned back. The moment of seriousness was broken, leaving a more relaxed sense of closeness between them. Her sense of being connected to him was stronger now.

"Like, I have this ocean diorama I've been working on since I was probably eight years old," she explained. "It started out as a school project, and then I just kept adding things to it—statues, shells, crafts I've made, models I've put together. The thing takes up almost an entire room at my parents' house. I add something new whenever I visit. My dad jokes he wants to turn the room into a gym or something, but he's added almost as much as I have over the years. Heck, one summer he even helped me make this colossal paper mâché squid for the midnight zone set up in the closet. The thing took us three months to finish. The next year, my mom and sister painted a mural on the walls. It's funny to think it all started with a shoe box and Play-Doh."

"Well, I don't have anything quite that large, but I do like to make animal figures." Eric picked up a thin piece of leafy vine. As she watched, he tied a series of knots. Within seconds, it took on the shape of a bird of prey. He handed it to her. "I make them out of whatever I happen to find while I'm out hunting."

"That's incredible." She twirled the tiny bird. It was solidly constructed, its wings made out of leaves. "I made a hedgehog out of a pine cone once, but it wasn't nearly this cool."

Eric laughed and thanked her.

When she reached out to hand the bird back, he closed her fingers around it. "You keep it."

They resumed walking at a more leisurely pace.

She smiled. "Thank you. How do you hunt, anyway? I mean, you said ... angelics take full animal forms, right? How do you avoid hunting one of them?"

"It's not really an issue," he answered, extending a steadying hand as she stepped over a large cluster of rocks. She accepted it, and watched her footing until they were back on flat ground.

"We have designated hunting areas, and besides, most Calaspians are a predator species. Of the few who are a prey species, most are demonic. There aren't very many prey angelics. Also, there's a spark, which is missing from any animal without a human soul. When you sense the spark, you know you're seeing a Calaspian."

He led the way carefully along the trees. Now that she wasn't in imminent danger, Nancy found herself fascinated by how different everything looked. There were colors she couldn't identify. She peered down dark paths, noticing curious glowing insects, and committed everything to memory. They walked in silence for a while, working together to lift low-hanging limbs and maintain balance when climbing rough terrain.

He anticipated her needs and offered a hand whenever she needed one. His pace matched hers. It was never too fast, despite his larger gait. She watched him move with ease, despite the fatigue she saw in the sweat on his brow and the increased rate of his breathing. From his movements, she could tell his shoulder was still causing pain, though he never complained aloud. Truth be told, she was tired herself, but if he was good to keep going, she wasn't going to say anything. She wasn't about to ask him to stop for a break when his brother was hurt and possibly dying. Rest would come later.

"There's a place up in the trees ahead where we can stop to rest. It's high enough that we should be safe for a while."

She looked up in shock. "Do you hear *all* my thoughts?" She was unable to avoid the question any longer. She wanted to know, but part of her was afraid of the answer.

Eric gaze was filled with compassion. "No, not at all," he assured her. "I would never intrude on your private thoughts without permission. I hear a few stray ones here or there that you accidentally send out."

"And that's how you knew I was tired?"

Eric laughed heartily and turned her to face him. Cupping her chin, he brushed hair from her face. "I know you're tired, because we're connected. What you feel, I feel." He searched her face and quietly read her. Eyes closed, he leaned in and pressed his forehead to hers.

A lump formed in her throat. She closed her eyes,

barely able to breathe. The air pulsed with charged energy. His hands didn't move from her head, yet she could swear they were caressing her body. He inhaled, and she exhaled. His pulse was her pulse. Through his mind, she glimpsed people like him, half hawk beings soaring over a forest canopy.

His arms curled around her waist and he lifted her. Wind rushed down her body and she quickly grabbed Eric's chest. Feathers emerged and covered his body, and she found leaves and limbs whirling past. Squeezing her eyes together, she clutched him more tightly.

Blood pumped so hard, the pounding resounded in her ears; she didn't realize they'd stopped moving until Eric removed his hands from her back and tilted her head upward. Cautiously, she opened her eyes. Hawk eyes stared back. Then, he blinked and they reverted to human eyes.

"Sorry about that. They change automatically when I fully transform. Better?" he asked with a soothing smile.

She nodded, unable to speak. Glancing around, she saw they were standing in an intersection of giant tree limbs that branched from a thick main trunk. Gulping, she looked down and wished she hadn't. Quickly, she tucked her head back into Eric's chest. "That's really high. Really, really high. So high," she murmured.

Eric's hand stroked her back comfortingly. "It's alright. I have you. You're safe. I promise."

Looking up uncertainly, she tried to slow her racing heart. Actually, she was dangerously close to hyperventilating. In the distant darkness, howls echoed. Her eyes widened. The phantoms! She was attracting them with her fear. She had to get hold of herself. Clenching his arms, she gazed across the vast expanse and then to the ground. She had to accept this height and not let fear control her. She breathed deeply and raggedly. Using the same techniques she employed to calm herself during breathing attacks, she returned close to normal. The howling grew quieter as the beasts moved further away. She kept a grip on his arms, but relaxed her hold. "This is really high." Her voice was devoid of emotion.

Eric's eyes reflected sympathy. "So you said. Here." He helped her sit down on a tree limb. Leaning back against the tree, he positioned her in front, his chest pressed against her back, his arms and wings around her. "I'm sorry I frightened you."

She shook her head. "It isn't your fault. I'm a total wuss with heights. So ... I guess this means your wing is better?" Her voice trembled. She wanted him to be better, but a good wing meant flying, which meant heights, which meant ... being up high. Her body shook.

"It's okay for this, but it still needs time before it's ready for full flight. Get some sleep. I have you."

Nancy nodded and tried to relax. With his arms and wings holding her tightly, she could almost forget how high she was. Almost. She straightened. "What if you fall asleep and let go?"

"I won't let go. I promise. You're safe here, with me."

And she believed him. She felt the conviction. It was so strong, she almost mistook it for her own emotion, but upon introspection, recognized that it was coming somewhere outside herself. Pursuing it, she was drawn to a nexus of other emotions. Concern. Regret. Caring. Fear. The more she pursued it, the more she sensed. What an intriguing revelation. He'd said he could detect her fatigue; he'd have felt her fear, as well.

Shifting, she curled up and lay her cheek against his feathered chest. His arms tightened, and she heard him sigh. As her breathing slowed, so did his. They really were somehow connected. "Tell me more about your world, your family."

Eric complied, stroking her hair as he spoke about each of his siblings and their families. "There is, of course, me and Ephraim. Then there's Ethan, Eagan, Elijah, and Evan."

"That's a lot of E's."

"Ha, that's not even all of them. Our mother's name is Evelynne." He grinned. "And a few of my brothers' children have 'E' names, as well. Ethan and Evan both have two children, all boys. Eagan has three girls, and Elijah has a mix, two girls and three boys. They range from ten years to — Evee was born eight months ago. That little crazy girl is already crawling. Landon and Kyrie started going on the hunts last summer, and Jean can prepare food dishes that rival my mother's." His voice beamed with pride and love.

"Your mother likes to cook?"

"Everyone loves when she cooks," he clarified. "You won't believe how much she cooked for Solstice this year. It's her favorite time of year. She always goes overboard, cooking more than any two people combined do. This time, I think she beat all her old records. She loves celebrations and feasts, and all the people and bustle. The more people surrounding her, the happier she is. Ever since my brothers began families, she's been a beacon of energy."

"What about you? Do you like all the people and excitement?"

Eric shrugged. "Not really. I mean, I love being around my family, but I spend most of my time alone or watching out for Ephraim. We do a good bit with our friend Narlic, but he's a fairly quiet person. He's a hawk angelic. His parents disappeared during the time of the witch trials and persecution, before the portals closed. He lost a few friends that way, too. All the hawk families tried to take him in, but he gravitated to ours. We tend to adopt people like that. He spent centuries on his own, keeping to himself before I met him. But I needed his help, and he was tired of being alone, so it all just worked out."

"What did you need help with?"

Eric took a deep breath. "I got tangled up in one of my own traps while hunting." Nancy suppressed a laugh.

"It's okay, you can laugh. I'm sure I looked ridiculous, fumbling around in that thing for half a day. Narlic found me, helped me out, showed me what I was doing wrong, and never told anyone about the entire incident."

"Wow, now that's a good friend."

He shrugged. "He knew I was trying to prove myself to my father and brothers. As the oldest, I felt like I needed to do it all on my own. But I needed help, and he provided it. So, once I had something to take back home, I invited Narlic to come to dinner with us. After all, I'd never have caught anything without him, so I felt like he should get to enjoy it, too. He hesitantly agreed and hasn't eaten dinner alone since."

"That sounds nice. I've never really had any friends like that. It's always been just me and my sister. I did have one friend when I was little, but she moved. We kept in touch with letters for a while, but I haven't seen her in years. The last time was kind of awkward. Neither of us had seen each other in so long, we didn't know what to talk about or do."

"Sounds like you spend a lot of time alone."

"I guess that's true." She hated being around people when she got a breathing attack. They were always concerned, trying to call an ambulance or take her to a doctor, or they tried giving her advice about how to endure it. They were trying to be helpful, but they usually just made things worse. "I don't mind. I like it when things are quiet and calm."

"Unlike today," he quipped.

Nancy laughed. "It hasn't been that bad."

"No, it hasn't been that bad, all things considered," he agreed.

"We'll get to your brother in time." She wasn't sure what had made her say that, but she could feel his gratitude, so she guessed he needed to hear that. He squeezed her gently and rubbed his chin against her hair, kissing her head.

They were quiet for several minutes. Eric's deep, even breathing nearly put her to sleep, but she still had so many questions. "I've been wondering ... the way you speak ... you said your people haven't been to Earth in hundreds of years, yet you talk just like anyone from here."

"We have a knack for languages," he explained, continuing to stroke her hair and hold her tightly, "especially ones we're already familiar with. It's a combination of instincts, telepathy, intuition, empathy, and our strong connection to and faith in the divine. Even when we don't understand all the words, we get a good grasp of what's being said. It makes us excellent at discerning deception. Also, those like my mother, with a strong connection to their home worlds, sometimes get insights and glimpses into changes that happen there. They perceive thoughts or memories, usually tied to intense emotions. That helps us pick up colloquial speech patterns and things like names."

"I think I must be going crazy." She ran her fingers over his chest, caressing the feathers.

"Why is that?"

"None of this sounds all that unbelievable, anymore. People who turn into animals? Sure. Magic rituals and time fluctuations? Why not? A bunch of immortals who can understand all languages? Seems plausible."

Eric chuckled. "Well, you're taking all this better than I thought you would."

"You thought I'd pull out the pitch forks?" She sensed his confusion and laughed. "Ah, so you *don't* understand everything I say." She pushed back to look at his face. He shrugged and waited for her to explain. "It's a reference to old movies. Made-up stories," she added, "that people act out for entertainment. The angry and afraid villagers go after the usually well-meaning monster and try to kill him."

"With pitch forks?"

"Generally, yes. And fire," she added. "They were big on fire."

"Ah, well, then yes. I was afraid you'd think me a monster."

"I could never think that," she responded simply. They shared an intense look, and she felt his desire to touch her. He remained still, however. She returned her head to his chest.

Eric breathed deeply, then kissed the top of her head, his body shaking from the effort of holding back.

"You mentioned a light coming to Earth," she prompted softly.

"Mmmm-hmmm. It was the magic of our connection, showing me where to find you. I felt it build in my chest and shoot toward the Earth portal."

Her heart sped up. "Can you still see it?"

"No, but I feel it."

She thought of the light and sense of connection that had overwhelmed her by the car. She'd experienced it again when they'd met. Now he was describing the same thing.

"You saw the light? I didn't think humans could see it,"

he mused aloud. "I'm sorry. I didn't mean to read your thoughts. It's just ... touching like this ... this is very different than I'm used to."

Nancy reeled from the one-sided conversation, unsure if she even needed to respond. It was strange having her thoughts heard, but she wasn't mad. It wasn't like he was doing it on purpose. His voice sounded nervous. He was afraid of upsetting her, of overstepping, and pushing her away. She felt his anxiety swell and then subside as he suppressed it.

"Eric, are you ... okay? I mean, with all the craziness, and your brother, and having to come to Earth ... it's okay if you're not ... okay. I know you feel a responsibility to every-one, to your family and friends ... to me. But you don't always have to shoulder the burden by yourself. We all have our own roles to play, our own experiences and talents to contribute to the journey. Accepting help doesn't show weakness. It just allows others to develop their strengths."

Eric swallowed heavily. "Old habits are difficult to break. I'm the eldest. It was my job to keep him safe, to protect him." He shuddered, closing his eyes upon feeling failure and fear. Finally, he stared off, into the distant trees. "I keep having this thought of having to tell my mother he ... he's ..." Eric choked.

Nancy took his hand and peered into his eyes. With complete conviction she said, "What happened with your brother is not your fault. From everything you've told me, he is a strong-willed, stubborn, *good* man ... just like his broth-er," she grinned. "He'll get through this and be stronger for it. And you'll be there, next to him, to help him with love and guidance, all along the way."

The burden eased from his eyes. He touched her face gently. The air pulsed, heavy and charged, as though every atom of their beings were in intimate contact. "Ephraim isn't the only one I want to protect."

She felt the air catch in her throat. "I know."

Eric placed his free hand over hers. "How about you? Would you also allow me to share your burdens? Time-shifting from your home, learning of new worlds and people, being asked to believe your soul mate is a half hawk, immortal stranger. Surely, there's something you wish to talk about."

"Well, when you put it that way," she laughed lightly. "I ... I don't really know how to put anything I'm feeling into words. Everything is just so crazy and fast. I feel like my head is swimming. Nothing makes sense, and yet everything makes sense, all at once." She looked at him solemnly. "I know I trust you."

Eric brushed her face again and smiled. "That means more to me than you can possibly know."

Nancy allowed her mind to wander, letting the words flow at random. "I feel like ... like I'm back in a band, playing my flute. There were times I'd be playing music, and I could *feel* it! It was like the music was alive, a part of me. And I was hitting super hard, fast notes and doing runs of scales perfectly. And then, I became hyper-aware, like I was waking from a dream, and all of a sudden, everything started to fall apart as I scrambled to keep up with the music ... feeling like I was completely disconnected to my body, like I was watching someone else's hands move.

"I could barely remember how to finger even simple, middle-of-the-scale notes. At some point, you have to let things flow around you, and flow with them without over thinking what you're doing. You have to trust, and let it happen, and see where it leads you." She leaned back, slipping her arms around his waist. "I'm trying not to over think things, to just see where this journey leads. I don't know what I think, or what everything I'm feeling actually means, but in this moment, in this place, I know I'm where I'm supposed to be. Is that okay?"

"That's perfect." With a tender smile, he resumed stroking her hair.

A strong wind blew, prompting heavy branches to sway. She grabbed him. "Are you really sure we're safe up here?" she asked, trying to ignore the returning fear of sitting so high up.

"I do this all the time," he answered, pressing his lips to her hair and keeping his face there, nestled close.

Trusting him, hearing the steady rhythm of his heart, she fell asleep.

———

TIGHTLY, Eric wrapped his wings around them. His arm felt surprisingly strong. His shoulder and wing were healing much faster than expected. As bad as the wing injury was, he should not have been able to fly up to this tree. The only time he recovered this quickly from an injury was when he saw a healer, of which there were none here. Then again, how was he to say how things here would move in their time-shift reality? Stroking Nancy's hair, he thought about everything.

The depth of her fear while flying up to the tree surprised him. So did her strength. She was terrified of being high off the ground, but she faced that fear, and she trusted him. The magnitude of that was astounding. She believed in him enough to sleep beside him, in this tree she was so afraid of. She had confidence in his ability to protect her.

Eric stared off into the trees and thought back to that first Solstice, the year he'd reached the age of maturity, the age where he could be mated. It was stormy that year. Mated females rushed around covering the festival area with tarps made of woven leaves and vines. His mother remained inside that Solstice, taking care of Ephraim and his brothers. Most of them had been young at that time. They huddled around the house, the winds thrusting open windows and repeatedly blowing out candles. They sang songs, ate a modest meal, nothing like the feasts she now prepared, and spent the day celebrating.

As the time for the magic drew near, his father pulled him aside, flying him through the rain, up to a branch with a cover of thick leaves. They sat and stared at the stormy sky in peaceful quiet for a long time. Finally, his father spoke. "It can be easy for our kind to take the finding of our mate for granted. We often meet and commit to them in a single day. There's no doubt or question as to who we're destined to be with. It's all handed to us on a platter. We rarely have to prove our love. There's no wooing or struggling to earn their trust, not like with humans." He smiled fondly, his mind far off, in a time long before. With a soft sigh, he continued to reveal his father's counseling.

"Love is not to be taken for granted. You have to earn it every single day. Your mate is like a precious gem mined from a mountain. Whether you have to toil hard and dig it from the rock, or find it easily outside in the sand, never forget how precious she is, and more importantly, never let her forget how precious she is to you. Make her know it. Make her feel it every single day. And remember that your mate is not your only gift. The love between you is just as precious and just as easy to take for granted. God is love. Wherever love is, God is. But God is also truth. He is both, *always*. Truth without love can be cruel. Love without truth can be selfish and equally cruel. But when you have both in the right balance, there is light and hope. We are beings of instinct and passion. Our emotions can run high. It can be easy to be overwhelmed, but your mate is your light in the storm. She is your center of calm and peace, if you allow her to be. She is a conduit of divine energy, and it is your job to be the same for her. The stronger your love, the greater a presence you allow God to be in your lives, and the greater your faith will develop. Lean on each other for strength and allow yourselves to grow together."

For years after that, his father provided the same speech. Eventually, as his brothers grew older and had their own time with their father for him to impart his Solstice wisdom, the time spent with Eric lessened ... with one exception. When Eric grew restless and frustrated waiting, his father took him aside and said, "You will be mated when you are both ready. Have faith. It will happen precisely when it is meant to happen."

Eric looked down at Nancy, asleep in his arms, and smiled appreciatively. Now, he understood why it had taken so long to be mated. She hadn't even been born when he'd received that first Solstice speech, but now the time was right. They were both ready. She may not have completely accepted all he'd said, but she felt it. Of that, he was sure. She felt their connection and a strong attraction toward him. She saw the light of the Solstice magic, which bound them. But *how* had she seen the light?

He stroked her hair and her body relaxed. Nancy. *His* Nancy. His mate. All the times he'd imagined how this day would go, he'd never imagined anything like this. Now, he couldn't imagine anything or anyone else. He could envision a life with her, enjoying her smiles, her laughter. He could picture their children and the many happy memories they'd share. Would their children have her eyes? He hoped so.

Letting his happy thoughts follow that train of thought, he closed his eyes and drifted off to sleep.

CHAPTER SEVEN

Gelick paced around the cave. He shifted from human, to panther, and back. Where were they? It shouldn't take his beasts so long to bring back one human soul. He sensed her out there. Her energy was enticing and strong.

A gash appeared on his arm. He eyed with idle curiosity, wondering where he would get that injury. After years of living in the sands and surviving, he'd learned to work with the peculiar energies of this realm. With his control over time fluctuations came strange side effects, wounds that appeared out of nowhere and disappeared once the injury actually occurred. He flexed his arm. While the gash looked bad, deep and raw, it didn't impede movement. It would heal. There were other things to worry about.

He watched the beasts crawl in from the shadows. They kept to the walls, staying as far from him as they could manage. When he stepped forward, they shrank back even more, stumbling over one another in an effort to retreat. A couple darted into the night. He regarded the remaining beasts as they limped and nursed injuries. "Where is she?"

One beast looked up defiantly. Gelick sensed great strength inside of him. This one had sampled her energy, but if he had her, where was she? How had she escaped? He closed his eyes and inhaled the scent of her life force. It was strong. While they always took a little when capturing his prey, the effects should have worn off by now. This beast had fed for an extended period, more than necessary to subdue the girl. Opening his eyes, he grabbed the creature by the neck. The other animals scattered to the far side of the room. "You know better than to take so much energy before bringing her to me."

Drawing on the beast's energy, he drained what was left from the girl and then kept drawing, taking all but the last vestiges of light. Memories and thoughts flowed through him. He viewed the girl, beautiful and strong, fighting and running. Then he saw the Calaspian, a hawk, swoop to her rescue. That was why the beasts had failed. The mates were no longer apart. They'd be more difficult to track and harder to fight. If he wanted the girl, he'd need to separate them. If he played this correctly, he could have them both, and once he secured the girl, the hawk would be crushed.

He absorbed more of the beast's memories and saw the portal the man had come through to enter Earth. That is where they'd be returning. That was where he'd set up the strike. Once he had them in the sands, they were his.

Gelick released the animal and walked away. It crumpled to the floor and whimpered. "Go to the portal," he commanded. "Wait for them there."

The beasts ran to comply. He thought back to the images of the girl. Something about her intrigued him. Images of another woman flashed through his mind. He tried to grab onto it, but it slipped away. Who was this woman, and why did she play upon long forgotten memories?

Looking at his arm, he noticed the wound was no longer bleeding.

———

TAP, tap, tap. The gentle sound of knocking awoke Nancy from a peaceful sleep. She found beautiful white and brown feathers surrounding her and, just past the wings, sat a small squirrel hitting a nut against a tree limb—or rather she thought it was a squirrel. It had bright green fur with an orange belly and glowing purple eyes. Otherwise, it looked like a squirrel. Tap, tap, tap, tap. The nut broke and the "squirrel" grabbed the pieces excitedly.

Underneath her, Eric's feather-covered chest rose and fell rhythmically. The bandage had finally fallen off, but he didn't need it. The cuts were almost gone. Tiny pink lines on the skin between golden-brown feathers were the only sign they'd existed. Feathers covered his biceps and forearms and stopped just above his hands, where scales lined the backs of his fingers. The hands were a strange combination of human and hawk; lines creased his soft palms and five fingers like a human, but each finger was tipped with a shiny black claw. His feet and legs were almost entirely hawk-like in appearance.

She looked at his face, studying every feature. From a distance, it appeared mostly human, but close up she could detect fine downy feathers that circled his eyes and followed his cheekbones. His nose and lips were human in appearance, and human hair topped his head. He was a perfect blend of hawk and man.

When she shifted, his arms tightened. True to his word,

he'd not let her go, even in sleep. She felt her eyes tear with gratitude. Could she really spend the rest of her life like this, waking up surrounded by nature, in the strong arms of a handsome man who cared for her and protected her, nestled against his soft, warm feathers? She smiled blissfully. Other than being up ridiculously high, it was perfect. *He* was perfect.

She thought back to his question. Which did she hope for? She hadn't known the answer then. She knew it now. She hoped this was real, that he was hers, and she could be part of his magical world and loving family. She wanted to be loved by this man in every way ... *she wanted Eric.*

Nancy longed to touch him. Hesitant fingers barely brushed his face. He groaned and pulled her closer, pressing his mouth to hers before she realized what he was doing.

Energy and excitement surged through her body. Eric's mind and emotions were garbled with sleep, and he wasn't fully aware of his actions. His body reacted to her touch on its own. This did nothing to limit the effect he was having on her; if anything, it heightened it. She felt his need and desire. Even though her mind told her she didn't know this man, her soul rejected the reasoning. She wanted his kiss ... and she wanted more.

Surprise coursed through him when he fully awakened. His lips pulled away with a ragged breath. His hawk eyes blinked several times as he breathed deeply to take hold of his emotions, conquering them, and controlling his desire and body. As he suppressed the emotions, hers lessened to a more manageable level.

Eric eyes changed from hawk to human when he met her probing gaze. Nancy felt a stab of guilt for having asked him to hide his natural eyes. They still made her uncomfortable, but that wasn't his fault. Eric hadn't done anything wrong.

Eric shivered and his entire body, save for the wings, changed back to human form. Chest still bare, he wore the pants she remembered from their first meeting. The awkward way he shifted his hips, coupled with ongoing desire and sudden embarrassment, and she understood his discomfort. When her lips curled with amusement, she felt the embarrassment intensity. Their emotions, feeding off and reacting to each other, suddenly made her head spin. Unsure how to sort them, she threw her arms around his bare chest and tightly embraced him. Listening to his beating heart, she tried to calm the storm within.

"You feel the emotional connection?" he asked quietly. His hands, cupping the back of her head, held her close to him.

She wanted to deny it, to keep that little gem to herself until she knew what to make of it all, but the intensity was too strong. She needed help. "How do you make sense of it all?"

She felt his compassion and understanding. Calming thoughts soothed her. His breathing slowed and deepened. "Better?"

She nodded with relief and sat back. "Does this sort of thing happen all the time?"

"Only with mates. We can pick up on the stray emotions of anyone really, and there are a few Calaspians who are naturally empathic, but with mates the connection is always there. It's always open." He clasped her hands in his and stared deep into her eyes. "And when we touch, the connection is even stronger."

Tender feelings of love and commitment flowed through her. Joy and gratitude enveloped her. Then

Nancy's mouth opened in surprise. Did Eric truly feel that strongly about her? And if she could feel all of that from touching hands, what would she feel if they were really intimate? What could he feel from her when she wasn't even sure she knew what she was feeling? "When we were walking, we held hands, but I didn't feel all this."

"You may have, but sometimes things can get lost before you learn to recognize them, and if you're feeling strong emotions yourself, they can drown out what you feel from others. As the connection between us strengthens, our ability to sense and understand things through the connection will intensify."

"I'm sure this makes for interesting arguments," she said wryly.

He laughed. "It's actually more beneficial than detrimental. When you can feel a person's motivation for saying and doing things, it helps give a different perspective. At least, that's what I've observed."

"But if you get angry, doesn't the other person feel that rage and then start feeling angry, too? How do you know which emotions belong to you and which ones belong to someone else? How do you know if what you're feeling is real and not just a reflection of what someone else is feeling? Can you even trust your own emotions?" Could she believe her feelings? What if they weren't hers? What if all her desire to be with him was a product of her tapping into his feelings? Would she ever know the difference?

Before she could continue, Eric pushed her onto her back and leaned over. His face hovered inches from her ear.

A breath caught in her throat. What would happen next?

"Sometimes it's obvious. Right now, you sense surprise, because I caught you off guard. I know that emotion is yours and not mine. Other times," he blew lightly against her neck, "the emotions are trickier. They can build off each other. But if you focus," he swept the tip of his nose along her ear, "you can pinpoint their origin."

Nancy found it difficult to focus. "And if you can't?"

"You get distance." Eric moved off and helped her sit up. He released her hands, and the emotional connection returned to its original intensity.

Nancy's body still shook from desire. She wanted to kiss him, but was that emotion hers or his? Confused, she rubbed her head.

"Now focus."

She did as instructed.

"What do you feel?"

Nancy thought again of the desire to kiss him and blushed with embarrassment.

"Good, focus on that feeling. Follow it."

She was confused for a second, then realized he was referring to her embarrassment. Doing as he directed, she tried to analyze everything she could.

"You know that emotion is yours. You felt its origin. It has a cause you can identify. It connects to other emotions inside of you. Now, this." He touched her hand again, and she was struck with a sudden desire to laugh. Unable to stop herself, and despite holding a hand to her mouth to suppress the feeling, she started giggling. She didn't know what was so funny, but whatever it was, it was hilarious.

Eric was grinned. "Do you feel the difference?"

"I, yeah," she forced through giggles, "I can't stop laughing." She doubled over. "But I don't know why. What ... what is so ... funny?"

"I'm thinking about my dad's last birthday party." His grin became a full-blown, toothy smile. "My oldest nephew wanted to play a trick on one of his brothers. He poured a large amount of seasoning into his drink. Only, one of my brothers drank it instead. He had a coughing fit, knocked over another glass of water on the table, which caused one of my nieces to jump up. She scrambled off the bench and fell into her mother, who happened to be bringing out the cake. It went flying and splattered across the table where the younger children were sitting. They cheered and tore into the cake with eager hands and mouths. Then, covered in bright blue frosting, they ran around the room, smearing frosting onto everything as their moms chased behind."

By the time he finished his story, Nancy had erupted into a full-blown belly laugh. "And that," he laughed along with her, "is what it feels like when you experience an emotion on your own, as well as having it heightened by someone who shares that same emotion." He removed his hand and she felt the need to laugh lessen. She still found the entire story humorous, but she could breathe again and not cry with laughter.

"Feel the difference?" he asked.

Nancy nodded. "I think so."

"It takes practice."

"How are you so good at it?"

"I'm not," he chuckled. "I know a few things, because I grew up with five younger brothers in a relatively small home. Whenever you're around anyone that much, you become attuned to certain things. But it was nothing like this." Eric smiled and shifted back into his full hybrid form, minus the hawk eyes. Slowly, he rolled his shoulder and stretched his wing.

"How does your wing feel?" she asked. "Wow, that's not a question I ever thought I'd ask."

"Good," he answered with a grin. "I should be able to cut down the remaining travel time substantially."

"By flying?" She kept her voice level, but her gaze widened; she couldn't hide the fear.

"It's the fastest way," he assured her quietly.

"Sure." She swallowed. Her skin turned clammy, and she felt feverish. "Not a problem."

Eric's eyes narrowed as he cocked his head, regarding her closely. "Come here." He stood and, taking her hands, led her to the edge of the branch. Nancy kept her eyes up, trying to avoid looking down. His hands now on her arms, he stood behind, his head over her shoulder. He spoke softly in her ear. "What do you hear?" Surprised by the question, she gazed back, and he nodded.

Closing her eyes, she focused on sounds she could pick up. Tap, tap, tap, tap, tap. "A squirrel trying to crack a nut." High up in the canopy, she could hear rain still coming down, though the leaves blocked most of it from falling here. "I hear the rain ... and the wind. The wind is blowing through the trees and making wispy, shuffling sounds."

"What do you smell?"

Taking a deep breath, she smiled appreciatively. "Flowers. Lots of flowers."

"What do you feel?"

"The moisture in the air. I feel the wind blowing and your hands on my arms."

"What do you see?"

She looked out at the trees. Leaves glistened with moisture. Vines with vibrant flowers trailed up tree trunks and along branches. Gnarled wood was twisted with intricate designs and patterns. She glanced down and felt the world spin. Dizzy, she lost her balance, but Eric's hands remained firmly on her, never letting her fall. She placed her own hands on top of his and held on, struggling to gain control. Concentrating on the sounds, smells, and feelings she'd noticed a moment before, she stilled the spinning to a light quiver. It was uncomfortable, but a lot more manageable.

"Are you alright?"

"I'll manage." She faced him. "Let's just do this before I chicken out."

"There's just one more thing," he paused to make sure he had her attention. "It's really better if I use my other eyes to fly. I can see sharper and farther, and ..."

"It's fine," she interrupted. "Do what you have to." Wrapping her arms around him tightly, her stomach lurched as he lifted off and flew them quickly through the trees. Her human eyes didn't discern much of anything. The world was a blur of color. Dizziness back in full force, she could only hang on and trust he knew what he was doing.

This was Eric. This is where he belonged, soaring through the air, free and unbound. He was a force of nature, and this was his element. And it terrified her. How could they be destined for each other, when something as core to him as this caused her apprehension? How could he ever be happy if he was unable to share such an important part of himself with her? She couldn't dismiss his claims of a connection between them. The attraction and emotional bond were impossible to ignore. Something was definitely pulling them together, but it was all wrong. *She* was all wrong. He was an incredible man who didn't deserve to be tethered to someone like her. He deserved to fly high with someone who could soar with him. Every moment he spent carrying her through the clouds, he was forced to experience her irrational fear. How many times could he do that before he grew resentful?

This wasn't fair to Eric. He didn't deserve to be

subjected to her fear, and it had to be a huge distraction to him, which also posed a safety hazard. If he became distracted, he could make a mistake, and they could both get hurt. Not to mention that every moment of fear was a beacon call to those beasts. She could do this. She *had* to do this. They were in the air either way. Being afraid wasn't going to change that. All it would do was make them miserable. She had to overcome the fear, but how?

She decided to focus on something nearby to take her mind off the height and speed with which they were traveling. Eric's wings provided the perfect distraction. He angled and soared through a break in the canopy. Once in the open, he was able to spread his wings out to their full twenty-foot span. They were an incredible sight. Every powerful flap took her and Eric a vast distance, propelling them through the air like a rocket. She let the movement become a type of visual meditation. She watched until time lost its meaning, and her fear of flight eased.

Just when she thought they would be flying forever, Eric took a dive. Squeezing her arms around him tighter than ever, she was unable to think of anything but her suddenly crushing dread.

"You can open your eyes," he said.

Only then did she realize her feet were on the ground. Nancy continued to cling to Eric. She didn't think she'd be able to stand on her own, should she let go.

Eric shed his hawk form and held her comfortingly. "You did great."

Nancy's body shook and she felt her face grow wet with tears. Hysterical laughter erupted. "Great? I have to be such a disappointment to you. Some soulmate I'd be. What a joke."

Eric clasped her face gently and peered intently. "Do you sense even an inkling of disappointment from me?"

Nancy scrutinized his smiling face, gentle and tranquil, and felt waves of acceptance and love. "Why would you want someone like me as your mate?" Her words were filled with uncertainty. "Your world terrifies me. I'm a coward."

"I've never known anyone braver than you in all my life," he said with absolute seriousness. Then, he kissed her passionately.

She felt fear and uncertainty melt. He loved her. He understood and felt her fear, recognized her weakness and, still, he loved her.

Nancy kissed with equal vigor. Pressing herself close, she felt the same desire stream through his body. He wanted only her. He desired her as she desired him. She knew she'd never feel for anyone else what she felt for him. Her senses sharpened. The world came alive with a symphony of sounds and sensations. Everything felt more real, more alive. Then, she sensed ... them.

Nancy pulled back breathlessly. They were approaching and she sensed the danger and the destructive vibration of their life energy advancing to surround them. "They're coming. But how can I know that?" she asked herself quietly.

"We have to run. The trees are too thick and dense to fly the rest of the way." Eric grabbed her hand and led her through a grove of trees. He remained human, but then again, human feet were better for running, and his wings wouldn't help him here. There wasn't enough room to spread them.

She could hear them now. The beasts were running, crunching branches, twigs and brush underfoot and sending assorted wildlife fleeing. She saw them sprinting through the trees. They were almost upon them. "I led them to us with my fear."

Eric lifted her over obstacles and urged her onward. "They were at this portal when I came through the first time. I was hoping they'd disperse before we got here ... but, no, this isn't your fault. They must have guessed we'd come this way, since it's the only portal around here."

"How far is it?"

"Not far." They broke through a copse and entered another grove. "You see that tree up ahead a couple hundred feet?"

"How could I miss it?" The energy encasing the tall tree was amazing. Light poured from every crack in the bark. The leaves glowed faintly along the veins, and beautiful flowers and braided vines wrapped the trunk and branches. The tree teemed with life.

"That's the portal. We have to go through the arch of that branch that curves back toward the ground."

A glimmer of diffused light reflected the air there. It reminded her of shimmering bubbles. She could see through it, but there was definitely something more substantive there. They ran through the arch and she felt intense energy prickle her body. Time stood still with that last breath she took before entering the portal. She felt pulled and lifted through countless images and sounds, but all passed so swiftly, she couldn't focus on any of them.

She saw a shadow of movement a split second before a beast rammed her side. Her fingers pulled free of Eric's hand, and she stumbled into a swirling vortex of energy. The last thing she saw before being thrown from the portal was a shadow beast on Eric.

CHAPTER EIGHT

Eric hit the ground hard, the wind knocked from his body. Bright sunlight blinded him. He braced for attack, but none came.

Eric felt raw with anxiety and anger. Nancy was gone. His mind was consumed by the last image of her as the beast knocked them apart. She could be anywhere, lost in the currents of time. He'd failed to protect her. Now, she was all alone, and it was his fault. His head and skin burned, as though his blood was boiling him alive. His vision blurred. He punched the ground where he'd landed and a cloud of sand shot up in his face, shocking him from his anger. This wasn't getting him anywhere. If he lost faith and became a fallen, there'd be no one to help Nancy and Ephraim. Things weren't over yet. He'd found her once. He could find her again. He just needed to focus and not let emotions run away with him.

His blood pressure lowered, and Eric pushed himself off the ground. Squinting against the blinding sunlight, he gazed around. Sand covered the land as far as he could see.

The phantom that had hit him was nowhere to be seen. It had likely been thrown to some other random place by the portal. That was good. It meant there was a fair chance the same thing had happened to Nancy. Wherever she was, maybe she was safe ... for the moment.

He closed his eyes and stretched his senses, easily feeling that energy he recognized as hers. Nancy was alive. He knew that much. She was confused, but not afraid.

Jumping up, he transformed himself and catapulted high into the sky, searching for a sign of his mate. Everything was quiet. The dust had settled. Flying higher, he stretched his senses again. She felt far away. He spun around, scanning all directions. Locating a bearing where her presence felt strongest, he took off at his fastest speed, propelling himself through the air. Focusing on his sense of Nancy, he flew so fast his hawk eyes could barely see. He pushed harder. There was no time for holding back. Nancy needed him, and time was not on his side.

———

IT WAS SUNNY. That was her first clue she was no longer on Earth. The world had been in a perpetual state of night-time since her shift out of phase. Was this Calaspia?

Nancy threw up an arm to shield her eyes. Sand lay everywhere, dotted by the occasional tree. It sparkled under the sunlight. She was in unfamiliar surroundings, alone. She gazed around through squinted eyes, but nothing that resembled the Calaspia from Eric's memories. So, where was she?

"It's all my fault," her mind cried. Anger and despair surged. Then, confusion displaced them. Why was she blaming herself? There was nothing she'd done wrong. Eric had said the phantom beasts were by the portal before. But still, she was convinced she was somehow to blame. The emotion didn't make sense. She couldn't pinpoint its origin. Unless ... Eric? He was blaming himself. He was angry and worried about her.

Nancy felt shock. Since they'd met, his emotions were calm, patient, and hopeful, even when talking about his brother. These emotions were different. They were raw and completely open to her. He wasn't holding anything back. It was a decidedly more human reaction than she was used to from him. He was moved to these intense emotions because of her, because they were separated. He cared that deeply for her.

A sense of tenderness was followed by concern. This wasn't good and it wasn't useful. She understood where he was coming from, but if he became too distracted, he could end up getting hurt by the beasts. He would draw them right to him. Besides, they would be okay. They would find each other and get out of here. But first, he needed to control his emotions and calm down.

As soon as the thought ran through her head, she felt his anger lessen. "I'm safe," she thought, hoping he could hear. They could do this. He'd found her across the worlds before. Only this time, she knew he was there and she wasn't alone. He was out there and they would find each other. She felt his emotions calm. He was responding. She was helping him.

Nancy took a deep breath and closed her eyes while she assessed the situation. She was alone in a desert with no visible cities or mountains, or anything else viewable in the distance. The sands of time. Eric had mentioned people being lost in the sands of time.

She let that thought sink in. Refusing to panic, she continued the assessment. There were two options. She could stay where she was, or move onward. With those phantoms out there, neither option was great, but they were the reason she was here. They might even know where she was right now. If she moved, there was always the chance of finding another sanctuary or, more importantly, finding Eric and getting out of here. But which way should she go? With a determined breath, she ran toward where the trees seemed the thickest, seeking the safety of cover. There wasn't much. Everything was open. None of the trunks were overly bulky and there was no foliage. This may be a magical desert, but it was still a desert. That trees existed at all seemed improbable, even impossible.

Her foot slipped on a slick spot, and she fell flat on her butt and back. Nancy winced and groaned. The place she'd slipped was hard and reflected the sun. She touched it. The ground felt like glass.

She noticed other glassy patches reflecting sunlight. She'd have to pay more attention. Dusting off, she stood and resumed her run.

———

"AND THAT MAKES THREE." Nancy stared up from the ground. Her sore butt rested on another glass-like spot. This wasn't working. Despite how far she had run, she could still make out where she'd started from. The branches of the tree towering over her blocked out most of the sun. Its lower limbs were nearly bare, but the upper ones were dense with leaves. They were where she needed to hide.

Placing a hand on the tree, she realized she had no idea what she was doing. She wasn't exactly a tree-climbing kind of kid. She'd tried once when she was five, but the height had scared her; that was when she'd had her first breathing attack, fell from the tree, and broken her arm. Her parents put her on lock-down, keeping her inside where they could watch her. Not that she blamed them. That first attack scared the heck out of her, too. From that point on, she gladly avoided any strenuous activity that could bring one on. She'd tried rock-climbing a few years back, at her sister's insistence, to overcome the fear of heights. It was indoors with air-conditioning, harnesses, and pre-cut hand and footholds that were easy to grab. There were safety mats, first-aid kits, and it all still scared her crazy. This, however, was quite different.

Wrapping her arms around the trunk, she jumped up and grabbed on with her legs. It took several minutes to move up more than an inch. Every time she pulled up, she slid further down.

Muffled howls caught her attention. Her head start was over. She needed to hide now. Digging her fingernails into the rough bark, she tugged herself up. Her body started to slip and she grabbed the sturdy trunk harder, holding on with sheer force of will. It was tortuous work, but she found a rhythm and pulled herself up to the first branch. She studied it for several seconds and decided it wouldn't work. There weren't enough leaves, and it was still too close to the ground to protect her from anything. She continued to climb, ignoring what the height was doing to her stomach. She could do this. She *had* to do this.

Toes and fingers angled for purchase. Her body ached from the strain, but she kept on, moving past several more branches. She looked up. Not much farther above were three solid branches that should provide the needed cover.

She climbed to the middle. One dizzying look down, and she scrambled to the lowest of the three branches. This one would have to do. She wasn't going any higher.

Awkwardly, she threw one leg over the branch and gripped the trunk, switching legs and placing her back against the tree. The effort, however, resulted in her catching a foot on the limb and nearly tumbling headfirst to the ground. Breathing heavily, she hugged the trunk and held on tightly. Rough bark bit into her palms, but she didn't care. She wasn't letting go.

She froze at the sound of movement. Shadows darted along the ground, barely visible through the dense leaves. She held her breath. Her toes were just beneath the leaves, but she couldn't chance moving and drawing attention. Then she felt it, the small bundle of twigs and leaves in her pocket. It was the small bird Eric had made for her. She turned it around in her fingers and relaxed. As the shadows moved away, she remained still.

Now that she was staying put, the stress of the run and climb finally caught up. It wasn't easy to keep her eyes open. She was completely worn out. Her body ached from having to constantly hold her position in the tree. Her chest hurt and her head throbbed. She even felt the beginnings of thirst and hunger. She'd not felt hungry on Earth after the time shift. Apparently, this place was different.

She didn't know she'd fallen asleep until her body awoke with a start. It was dark. The sun had finally set. With it came a drop in temperature. Frigid winds blew across her exposed skin. She rubbed her fingers together and gasped when she realized the bird was gone. Frantically, she checked her pockets and looked around, but there wasn't enough light to see too far or anything on the ground.

She didn't climb down so much as fall—in an uncontrolled, sliding, flailing manner to land butt-first on the ground. She wiped the dirt from numerous cuts and scratches. Most were on her hands, but she felt several long scrapes running up her forearm. Her legs were sore, too, but her pants had mostly protected them.

She felt around the ground. Still unable to see much, she could make out a little, but she didn't spot or feel the bird. Her hands shook. It had to be here. She spun and a busted tree branch cut her arm while the wood left splinters in her finger. Still no bird.

Tears speckled the ground as she sobbed silently sitting against the tree. With the cold dark night surrounding her, she was chilled, numb, and alone. She didn't know how much time had passed on Earth. Did anyone know she was gone? Maybe it had been months or years for them. Were they still alive? Maybe everyone she knew had lived the rest of their lives wondering what had happened to her ... only to die, never knowing.

Was Eric still alive? The beasts could have found him. Or maybe he'd found a way back to his home, renounced their mating, saved his brother, and moved on with his life. She could be alone forever. Not forever, she amended glumly, just until she froze to death, got eaten by phantoms, or died from lack of food and water. Seemingly in answer to the thoughts, she heard a plaintive growl. In the darkness, a shadow shifted.

———

ERIC WAS YANKED from the sky by a sudden and overpowering burst of despair. It assaulted his body and mind, distracting him to the point where he failed to anticipate wind shifts. Blown aside, he collided with rock and fell, rolling to a stunned stop in the sand.

The land was covered with an eerie purplish haze. Still dazed by the emotions coursing through him, he peered around to get his bearings. Sand, heavy and thick, pelted his face. Blood pumped in his ears. His eyes burned and watered so much, the edges of his vision blurred.

Through the winds, he heard a faint scream. Stumbling upright, he moved in its direction. Cresting a hill, he saw the source of the scream. A man crawled in the sand, besieged by phantoms, struggling in vain to get away.

Eric jumped down and batted beasts away. They snarled and ripped at his skin, pulling off feathers and leaving dark red gashes. He stood his ground. Seeing his strength and determination, the beasts soon backed away. Eric watched them fade into the shadows before he turned to examine the man.

Frail, barely a pile of bones covered by skin, he looked up at Eric with a mixture of gratitude and fear. Sensing the man's human nature, Eric shed his hawk form and knelt beside him. The man's face visibly relaxed upon seeing Eric's human form. "Hello, friend. I'm Eric."

"Mia," the man said with a raspy voice. He tried to sit up, but given the weakness of his limbs, all he accomplished was a few inches of movement. "I have to find her. I have to get back to her."

"Is she here?" Eric looked around, but saw no signs of another human.

"Mia." He placed his head back on the ground and cried. "We were meeting at the lake, but I never made it there. I cut through the woods. I should never have gone there. I knew the stories, people disappearing without a trace. But I was impatient. I was going to propose." From his pocket, he pulled out a simple gold band with a small clear stone. "I was preparing what I would say and slipped, and fell down an embankment to this ledge. The air, it shimmered. I touched it, and I was here, wherever here is."

Eric's mind filled with sadness. This man was a human, lost in the sands, confused and alone, torn from his love, who would never know what became of him, whether he lived or died. With the way time moved here, she could already be dead, or perhaps she still waited at that lake for her love. "This is a place between time and space."

The man coughed, his face sporting a deathly pallor. He no longer tried to move. "I was going to be a father," he said softly. "She'll think I abandoned them." His last words were but a whisper. The man's eyes closed and the ring fell from his hand.

The winds howled. Lightning struck a rock fifty feet away. The man's body dissolved into bone and then dust. Shocked, Eric stared at his dust-covered hands until the wind carried that away as well. The glint of metal in the sand was the only evidence that the man had ever existed.

Eric felt ill. The despair that had knocked him from the sky amplified ten-fold. Here was a man who had had a lady love, and she had been taken from him. For what reason? Why should Eric, or anyone else, deserve more than that man? Why should fate twist and turn to bring Eric to his own love, or fulfill his desires of family any more than they had this nameless stranger? Because he was Calaspian? That didn't make him any more worthy or deserving of a happy life. But if God could use the tragedy of that man for a greater good, Eric could easily be used in just the same way.

The man's words haunted him. "She'll think I abandoned them." If something happened to Eric out here, that was what would happen to Nancy. She'd be lost and abandoned, only she wasn't at home, surrounded by her family and friends. Nancy would die alone. She could die before he ever reached her. He couldn't let that happen. With all the ways she could suffer running through his head, Eric took to the sky.

CHAPTER NINE

She was all alone. Who had she been kidding? She couldn't protect herself in this world. She couldn't even control anything in her life on Earth. What hope was there of positively influencing her life here, where the normal rules of existence didn't apply? Nancy pressed her face into crossed arms and let the tears flow.

Her body shook. None of this was fair. Life wasn't fair. Life wasn't good. Life was hope for a future you were never going to have. It was gazing around at all the suffering and believing, arrogantly, that you somehow deserved better than everyone else. "Why am I here?" she screamed into the darkness. "Why bring me to this place just to let me die?"

Nearly ready to give in, Nancy's leaned back on her hands ... and felt it ... the familiar feel of the bird figure. Like that, her fear vanished. A calm settled over her. She was experiencing Grace, she realized with awe.

As Nancy stood and took a deep breath, hope renewed within. Eric was looking for her she knew with certainty. She had to trust and believe that. She stared bravely into the shadows. The growls had moved farther away. That bolstered her confidence. She must keep moving. The creatures already knew she was around here. Now, with her recent temporary breakdown, they'd be sure of it. Hiding in the tree wouldn't protect her for long. Though she couldn't see much, she began walking. She may not be able to see more than a few feet in front, but that didn't matter.

Nancy always believed herself to be fairly spiritual. She believed in God. She believed things happened for a reason, or she tried to. It wasn't always easy. When her breathing attacks were bad, or life was generally unpleasant, she fell into doubt, but things were different this time. She'd found sanctuary when she'd needed it. She'd been led to that church where Eric had found her. She believed that. She felt that. Finding the bird figure in her moment of despair was a sign. She wasn't alone. Forces bigger than herself were at work here. She always believed God was with her. Now, she felt it. No matter what time, world, or realm she found herself in, she knew God was with her. Even if everyone she knew were gone, she'd keep fighting. She'd follow this journey to its end and trust things would ultimately work out for the best.

She began praying and singing in her head as she walked. She mouthed the words but kept silent so as not to be heard by anything hiding in the darkness. "T'was Grace that taught my heart to fear, and Grace my fears relieved. How precious did that Grace appear the hour I first believed." She hummed the words she didn't know and kept thinking of relevant and inspirational words to keep her going. "Yeah, though I walk through the valley of the shadow of death."

Looking pointedly to the unknown, she held her head

up defiantly. "I will fear no evil," she finished the prayer confidently. She would *not* fear this place. She'd not fear the dangers. Whatever struggles she had yet to endure would come when they came. Right now, she was alive ... and she would walk.

She took a deep breath. Her chest burned, but that was okay. She could do this. If she stayed calm, she could get through this. Eric would be looking for her. She just needed to stay safe until he found her. She had done it before and she could do it again.

———

ERIC CONTINUED TO FLY, even as the sky darkened and the strong winds grew colder, blowing sand against him like a thousand tiny needles and piercing his skin. He pushed through, ignoring the pain. Keeping one arm raised, he shielded his face from the onslaught. His skin tingled, the air vibrated around him, and a bolt of lightning shot downward, inches from his wings. He spun and saw it strike the ground with a loud bang. A tower of glass shot up. He gazed around and noticed several similar towers and slick places scattered about the terrain.

Avoiding another bolt of lightning, he focused his attention on any changes in the air that might warn him of another strike. His flight evolved into meditation. Duck, roll, fly up. His anticipation of the strikes increased. Then, the storm grew worse. Winds increased. Purple and pink light flashed behind ominous turquoise clouds. Eric navigated as best he could, but a few strikes came close. He anticipated the next strike and adjusted his flight, but wind gusted beneath his wings and threw him off course. Spinning, he struggled to right himself. Only years of experience flying and raw willpower kept him in the sky, but he nearly lost his bearings. Nancy, however, kept him on course.

A flash of light revealed a wall of rock just ahead. Angling up and back, he flew in a loop, coming to rest on a small stony ledge. His hand gripping the wall, he peered up through piercing rain into the night. This mountain rose out of nowhere. A blink later and he'd have flown straight into it. He saw the top. Taking a moment to catch his breath, Eric then leapt into the sky and flew to the plateau. He scanned the night. There was very little to be seen. Rain drowned out any light he might have had from the moons or stars.

Flying in these conditions was beyond dangerous, worse than the cave Ephraim had fallen in. The logical thing to do was find a safe place to wait out the storm, but every moment he waited, Nancy was out there alone. Lightning struck a blossoming bush by his feet. Before his eyes, it aged in reverse, changing into a single sprout.

His mind advised him to seek shelter, but his spirit cried out to brave the storm and find Nancy. What should he do? If he got himself killed, he couldn't help anyone, but he was more than willing to face any danger to protect her. What should he do, and why was he so conflicted?

———

WALKING EVOLVED INTO MOVING MEDITATION. Nancy trekked and prayed until all her previous fear had subsided, so much so it now felt almost unreal. It was strange how feelings could change so quickly.

Now that she was calm, thoughts turned back to Eric.

Nancy knew he'd do anything to protect her. They'd known each other such a short time, yet already he was undeniably important to her. He'd said they were soulmates. She had a hard time arguing with that. She felt the intense attraction he'd spoken of, the emotional connection. She wanted desperately to see him again, to feel his comforting arms around her, to hear his soothing voice. Both his human and hawk forms called to her on a level she couldn't explain. They were practically strangers, yet she felt she knew Eric's every essence.

He'd also said she'd gain his ability to transform. What would it would be like to change forms, as he did? Much to her surprise, the thought sparked an excited feeling of anticipation. How her body and soul ached to be with him. She wanted to share all her thoughts and questions. She wanted to play games and be in his company. She wanted to feel what it would be like to *not* hold back, to commit herself entirely to this marvel between them, and see where it would go.

When she'd stared out at the airplanes, yearning to jump on one and leave her old life behind her, she'd never imagined anything like this. But here she was, staring out at a new life with new possibilities. It was getting harder to hold on to the past. She wasn't even sure she wanted to anymore. What did that life hold for her? She'd been ready to leave it at the airport, and that was with far less motivation. Now, she had an idea what she'd be leaving it for. There was a destination, a life waiting, family and love.

It was a large leap of faith. Was she a person who believed in faith and love and trusted in God and her own instincts, or was she a person who let fear and uncertainty lead to a life of safe predictability? Which person did she want to be? She knew the answer. The real question was did she have the faith to be *that* person? If all he'd said were true, she'd become immortal. Immortal. How could her mind fathom such a thought? Was Calaspia like Heaven? Were they like angels? He'd said they weren't; they were simply named after angels and demons by humans, but she couldn't discount the similarities. They had faith, strong faith, and when they committed evil acts, they were cast out. When they lost faith, they fell. But they lived, had families, experienced joy and pain.

Eric worried about her still. She sensed it. He was worried even now—no, it was stronger than worry. He was *afraid*. Stopping mid-step, Nancy dropped to her knees and put her hands together. She focused on Eric and his fear, and imagined waves of soothing calmness washing over him, eroding the fear. Faith, not fear. They would get through this, together.

———

HE WASN'T afraid for himself, but for his loved ones, those who depended on him. If he sheltered himself somewhere, he feared leaving Nancy to face this world alone. If he flew, he feared being rendered powerless to help her. He couldn't make decisions like this. Whatever he did, he was reacting to fear, not trusting his instincts and following where they led.

Eric inhaled deep and centered himself. All around, the storm continued to rage. Whirling winds screamed through the darkness. Thunder shook the air and ground. Eric inhaled again, slowly and calmly, and assessed the situation. If he flew into the darkness, he could fly into a mountain or be struck from the sky by lightning. But the lightning really wasn't a problem. He already knew how to anticipate it, if he focused and paid attention. That was manageable. Almost to prove his point, lightning struck the spot where he stood—fortunately, he'd sensed it in time and stepped aside. It hit the rock.

The squally wind wasn't a problem, either. While strong winds could be dangerous, he was a strong flyer and good at correcting his course. It was also a manageable threat. That left the darkness. If only he could see a little more of his surroundings to plot a safe course.

Lightning lit up the entire sky, revealing shadowy peaks and rough terrain. His eyes committed everything to memory. As the sky grew dark, he stretched his wings and took to the sky. With thoughts of Nancy and Ephraim spurring him on—and a calm, centered, confident mind—he flew onward.

———

SHE STAYED LIKE THAT, kneeling in silent prayer, for a long time, until ice began to collect on her skin, and her breath came out in puffs of white clouds. Why did it have to be so cold? Nancy rubbed her arms to generate warmth. Her fingers rubbed cuts and bruises, but she barely felt them. Her skin was too numb. In an effort to distract herself, she resumed walking and tried to think of more songs. Very quietly, her voice raspy from lack of water, she sang a verse of "Father Abraham" and was halfway through the second verse, mostly making up the words she could no longer remember, when lightning lit up the sky and struck a nearby tree. Flames erupted and spread to a large pile of dead leaves.

Nancy ran to the fire, collecting twigs and adding them to help the fire grow. Clearing the surrounding ground so it wouldn't spread, she warmed her freezing body. Once feeling returned to her fingers and face, she sighed gratefully and leaned against a tree. Now that she wasn't moving, exhaustion started to take hold. Closing her eyes, she slept.

———

EPHRAIM LOOKED UP. Surrounded by rocks, water, and howling wind, he flinched at the pain racking his body. Everything hurt. He saw a shadow at the top of the cave. Eric, he'd get him out. He'd get help. Brilliant light streaked through the air and Eric was gone.

Ephraim blinked. That had been the light of Solstice magic. Eric was caught in it, unable to return and help until the mating was completed. "Just great," he grumbled, and wished he hadn't opened his mouth. Painful coughs assaulted his body. There was no telling how long Eric would be gone, and a quick scrutiny of the area proved no friends or family were close enough for a telepathic call for help, at least not with his current level of concentration. Throbbing pain made it difficult to see straight, let alone focus thoughts.

Around him, everything buzzed with energy. The wind grew instantly quiet. Water droplets hung motionless in the air. Ephraim stared in wonder, half sure he'd died and this was some transition plane. Then, a shock wave of light soared through the place. His vision was blinded by it. As it faded, he looked around in shock. He was no longer in a cave. Instead of cold rocks and water, he found himself lying in foliage. Flowers and leaves completely surrounded him. He tried to move, but the pain was still too great. Dizziness overcame his already fuzzy brain, and he fell unconscious.

———

GELICK APPROACHED the young girl as she slept. Beside her, the fire was nearly dead, not that she needed it. With the rising sun, the temperature was much more pleasant.

This one had proven a challenge to locate. She wasn't consumed by fear, as he'd predicted she would be, as most people in her situation would be. She was alone, stranded, and still she carried on bravely. Even the shadowy night and fierce storm hadn't ruffled her enough to give him more than a cursory indication where she was. It had taken his beasts an entire long night of searching to locate her. They'd probably still be searching if she hadn't stopped to rest. This one was special. Her energy would be worth the wait.

Gelick took a few more steps forward and paused. The closer he got, the more he felt an odd sense of familiarity. There was something about her that intrigued him. The tilt of her head, the slope of her jaw, the way her hair fell around her eyes, all spoke to distant memories. He closed his eyes, trying to hold on to the fragments, but they darted from his grasping mind.

The beasts shifted restlessly. They felt another burst of life energy traveling between the worlds and longed to chase it. With a slight mental push, he commanded them to stay. This girl was his prize, and he would need them.

Gelick looked at the thin line of scabs on his arm. The gash had nearly healed. He'd be in a fight soon. Could the girl be the one to injure him? He'd need to proceed with caution from this point on.

———

SHE AWOKE to the sound of muted growling. Sitting up, Nancy looked around and noticed faint shadows wavering in the light, approaching from all directions. In their midst stood the tall shadow of a man covered by a dark hooded cloak. He approached in jumps, but it wasn't like he was actually jumping; he moved every time she blinked. The shadow was fifty feet away ... then twenty. Then, he stood over her. In a matter of seconds.

"There you are." His voice was rough and cracked, as if from disuse. Another jump and he was on top of her, pinning her to the tree.

"What the ..." Nancy struggled, but he was strong and held her firmly in place.

He leaned in close, eyes narrowed. He studied her, smelling her neck and hair. She shuddered in revulsion as his nose passed but an inch from her face. "Why, it's you," he said in surprise. "My dearest, Adeline."

Her eyes widened. "I'm not—"

"But why were you traveling with that hawk?" His face darkened with anger.

She blinked with the rage-filled force of his question. "I'm not who you think I am."

His eyes narrowed even more as he continued examining her, considering her words. "You look so much like her." He stared at her necklace. Confusion twisted his face and his eyes glazed over as he inhaled sharply.

Pressure expanded in her chest. She felt as though her body were being pulled apart. The pressure traveled up her throat and out her mouth when she attempted to scream in pain. It was the worst pain she could remember, but she couldn't make a sound. Tears streamed down her face. Her body felt heavy and useless, and she was completely helpless to fend off the assault. It was like what the phantoms had done to her, only much more intense. He was *killing* her.

She had to fight. And Eric had to survive. He'd locate her, but she had to buy him time. Willing her body to move, she pulled up a knee and hit him as hard as she could. As heavy and out of sorts as her body felt, she wasn't entirely sure how hard that was, but the grunt of pain suggested it was good enough. She rocked back and forth, throwing him off her, and stumbled to wobbly feet ... then almost fell to the ground. Her initial burst of adrenaline nearly spent, she was left with weakness, exhaustion, and a numb feeling of being disconnected from the rest of her body. Moving with sheer willpower, she kept going. A surge of energy charged her from somewhere outside herself. Eric, she realized. He was coming. He'd find her. She *had* to survive.

Beasts raced around her, caging her in. She pushed past them, ignoring the pain as they bit and clawed her body. The man appeared in front of her. She stumbled back and turned, but he was there too. He moved faster than she could see, faster than time. Ducking as he reached for her, she came around behind and jumped up to grab a tree branch in an attempt to pull herself up. She didn't get much of a chance. He grasped her leg and yanked her back down. Her head hit the ground with a loud crack. She was down with no fight left, energy sapped, and breathing labored.

She watched with unfocused eyes as he hovered. Blinking in an effort to focus, she heard a muffled cry and felt a cool wind blow past. Talons grabbed the man's arm and pulled him away. With the next blink, the shadowy man was gone. A cloud of sand filled the air and filled her lungs. She coughed weakly, barely having enough energy to do that.

And then she was weightless, with air swirling around

her and the sky flying past. Sand dunes and shadows passed at dizzying speed. She struggled to move her head, but there was no strength left in her body. Letting her eyes drift closed, a feeling of peace came over her. She felt safe. Protected. Loved.

CHAPTER TEN

"**W**here are you, Nancy?" Cindy wondered aloud. It wasn't like her sister to be out this late without calling. Trying her cell phone again, she was sent straight to voice mail ... which was full, of course. She sent her a quick text and put the phone back in her pocket.

With a sigh of annoyance, she picked up the clothes hamper and made her way to the laundry room in the mid-sized apartment complex. Throwing clothes into an empty washer, she filled the soap dispenser, inserted the coins, and turned the switch. Nothing happened. Outside, a vivid flash of light filled the sky. Cindy swayed, suddenly feeling light-headed. Confused, she strolled to the window and looked at the night sky, expecting to see a thunderstorm. Instead, she saw strange swirling light alternating from blue, to purple, to pink.

A loud crash sounded outside. She scanned the shrubs and walkway, and gave a start. A trough near the building had been knocked aside, and something large was lying in a row of rose bushes. Cautiously, she walked outside. A peculiar feeling of anticipation streamed through her. There were low moans coming from the bushes. "Hello?" she called out worriedly.

As she approached, she could see a man, cut and bruised. "Hello?" she called out again.

He opened his eyes and stared straight. "You're beautiful," he said weakly, awed.

She felt her gaze transfix on his. "I'm Cindy," she replied softly.

He smiled. "Ephraim."

His eyes closed, and she shook off the strange feeling she experienced looking at him. "I'll get an ambulance," she promised and dialed the number on her phone, only nothing happened. There was no dial tone. She eyed the phone in confusion. "What's going on?"

A visible shiver ran across the man's body and he changed. Feathers covered his skin. His legs bent back unnaturally, ending with clawed bird feet, and wings sprouted from his back.

Cindy's phone fell to the ground.

Shaking off the shock, she examined him closer. He bore even more injuries in this form. He obviously needed medical help, but there was no way she could take him to a hospital. She'd have to help him. Lifting up his shoulders, she was surprised by how light he was. It wasn't easy by any means, but she was able to half drag, half lead him to the apartment. She dropped him gently on the floor and began working on his numerous injuries.

ERIC'S HEART continued to pound in his chest. Putting as much distance between them and the beasts as he could, he didn't slow down until he was sure the immediate danger had passed. Spotting an area of the desert where sand was peppered with crumbling boats and planes, he landed.

Gently, he lowered Nancy to the ground. His arm cradled her head as he examined her body. What he saw made him gasp with shock. Her arms and face were covered with cuts and scrapes, and her hair was matted with blood. Her lips were pale, dry, and cracked. There was very little color in her skin; she appeared frail and beaten. "Nancy?" he called softly.

Her eyes opened and she blinked several times before focusing on him. Her gaze locked on his, and her face lit up. "Eric!" she cried out in a raspy, dry voice. She hugged him tightly, with far more strength than he'd have thought her capable of. Tears wet his neck where her face rested. "I knew you'd find me," she whispered. He heard her through thoughts more than with ears.

Eric's heart warmed at her words and intense joy flooded their emotional bond. Afraid of hurting her, he gently hugged her back, grateful beyond words to have her in his arms again. At the moment, this embrace was all he craved. The sexual tension that filled them both whenever they were within close proximity currently lay beneath the surface. It had been replaced by something far stronger. He desired Nancy in his arms, his life, and by his side—he desired her presence, soul, mind and spirit, her laugh and voice, her scent. He felt a similar desire rage inside her. She clung to him like a child clinging to a precious blanket, as if he were everything to her. Eric regarded her with breathless awe.

Nancy touched his wing, brushing his feathers, enjoying the sensation. They traveled to his back. Warmth radiated from her fingers as they lightly stroked his sore muscles. They stopped on the bulging muscles that controlled the movement of his wings. The twinge of pain prompted him to suck back a quick breath. Warmth instantly filled the area, easing his muscles and letting them relax. He felt her desire to help him, to comfort him in some way.

"Have you been flying this entire time?" she asked quietly.

He shrugged, surprised how much better his back felt.

"That had to be pushing it, even for you. Did you fly in that storm?"

"It wasn't so bad."

"There was so much lightning! That couldn't have been safe. What if—"

"There's nothing I wouldn't face to find you."

Nancy tightened her arms around him, but this time he noticed they were lacking strength. The adrenaline spike from seeing him had worn off. Nancy was weak and injured. And now that they were together, Eric's own exhaustion had started to make itself known. He'd have given in to it if not for Nancy. He had to be strong for both of them. They weren't out of danger yet.

The wind picked up, blowing sand all around. Nancy started coughing and covered her face protectively with an arm. He took her hand and led them to the side of a nearby wooden ship. Nancy stumbled and nearly fell. Eric scooped her up and hurried inside the rickety ship, but it offered only moderate cover from the powerful wind. Sand swirled in the darkened hull, making it difficult to see and breathe.

Feeding her energy he could barely spare, he set Nancy on her feet and saw her steps grow stronger, her movements sturdier. She was still weak, but she could move. It would have to do.

She studied him closely. "You're helping me."

"Just a bit," he admitted. "I have a feeling I'm going to need your assistance finding a way to close up that breach."

She nodded.

He got the feeling she wanted to argue that he keep his strength instead of sharing it, but she couldn't argue with his reasons. Eric changed into human form to move more easily around the small space. Quickly and quietly they worked together to unfold a tarp and assemble it over a gaping hole and block sand from blowing inside. Light shone through the tarp, casting a reddish hue.

Nancy took a ragged breath and sank into the sand. Dust swirled in the air, making her cough. "Where are we?"

"The sands of time," he answered. "Otherwise known as Allegretarde. This is where things and people who get lost in time wind up." He patted the side of the ship. "Sometimes entire vessels find themselves lost here." He regarded Nancy, quietly sitting with her back to the wall. Her breathing was shallow and strained, but as weak as she appeared, he felt strength inside her. Gone were her feelings of confusion and uncertainty. She felt calm and at peace.

Her hand rested on her chest and clutched in her fingers were a bundle of twigs and leaves. His eyes widened. She held the bird he'd made for her. Not only did she still have it, she'd managed to hold on to it through everything, even while unconscious.

"That man was like the phantoms, only stronger. The beasts were working with him, like he controlled them. Was he a banished?"

"Yes." Eric knelt beside her and took her free hand. It was clammy, the skin dry and scaly. "And an exceptionally strong one. I've never heard of any who could keep their human form for long. He must have incredible willpower."

"Is that how he could see me? I mean, are we still out of phase?"

"This is Allegretarde," he shrugged. "Rules of time don't apply here. Everyone who exists in this realm has to deal with time fluctuations. Things speed up, slow down, reverse. Time isn't linear here. It gives people a different perspective or sensitivity that those in other worlds don't have." He slowly ran a hand through her hair, checking the injury from her fall. "And yes, we're still out of phase."

She flinched and closed her eyes. "That explains how he was moving, I guess. It was so fast, like time was moving and I couldn't see it."

"That would be why," he agreed. The head injury was bad, but seemed to be healing quickly, at Calaspian speed. He stretched his senses. The hawk was there in her, but it didn't feel strong enough for this level of healing, not yet.

"He called me Adeline." Her voice was barely a whisper now. "He acted like he knew me. The weird thing is, I have this family heirloom, a necklace, with that name on it." She pulled the necklace from beneath her shirt.

Eric touched the pendant, amazed. "Volimare metal!"

"What?"

"This is Calaspian," he explained. "May I?" She nodded and he removed the necklace and other chain, and put them on. Then, he changed into hawk form. The Adeline necklace remained visible, but the other chain disappeared. He changed back to human form and took off both necklaces, handing them back. "Only volimare, from Calaspia, has the ability to remain during a transformation. Pendants like this are actually quite common there. Many families carry them as a reminder of their clan and heritage. This is particularly true for those who spent a great deal of time on Earth." He regarded her closely, a thought forming.

"Why is that?" She blinked, her eyes heavy. Her mind focused on his words, but her body was on the verge of giving out. He fed her more energy and watched her straighten slightly. Her eyes cleared and she offered a weak smile of thanks.

With a nod, he continued. "On Calaspia, the metal simply stays visible during transformations. On Earth it serves as a power boost. Some Calaspians, who spent a lot of time on Earth, found secondary abilities developed. Wearing volimare has been known to increase the intensity of such abilities."

"What could they do?"

Eric thought. "Usually, it was enhancements to existing physical or mental abilities. I've heard of some gaining knowledge of future events or control over weather. Some of the ... powers ... are unusual and incredible, but most of the actual abilities are just variations of, or special focus on, things all of us can do to smaller degrees with practice and time."

"And this only happened to those who traveled to Earth a lot?"

"Mostly. Some abilities evolve on Calaspia, but not as many. There aren't a great deal of dangers or threats to warrant the need. But, on Earth, survival is not as ... guaranteed."

"That makes sense, I guess. Necessity is the mother of invention. Without challenge, there's less growth." Nancy shook her head and rubbed tired, dry eyes. Her cracked bottom lip displayed a thin line of red. "Okay, but what does all of that have to do with me? Why would my family have a Calaspian necklace? I get that there are probably some of these floating around, but I didn't pick it up at a garage sale. This is an heirloom. It's been in my family a long time."

He raised an eyebrow and waited for her to formulate what he'd already figured out.

She blinked and gasped. "You think my ancestor was Calaspian?"

Even with all the emotion he felt behind her question, and all the energy he continued sending through their connection, her body was still looking more pale and frail by the second. Something was very wrong. Eric considered taking them somewhere else, somewhere she could get food, or water, or help, but the wind outside wailed furiously. The makeshift door they'd put up whipped and twisted, bits of sand blowing in around the corners. They weren't going anywhere for a while.

Sliding closer, he took her hand. He was missing something. Perhaps the answer to his questions lay in figuring out her connection to his world. He'd not seen her necklace during their time together in the woods. There was a reason it had been brought to his attention now. This was important. "Do you know anything about this Adeline?"

"Just that she was found by a lake. She was injured, with no memory of ... of where she came from." Her eyes widened. "She was a fallen?"

He nodded, agreeing that assessment sounded the most likely.

"What does that make *me*?"

Eric was startled by the question. What did that make her? His heart began to race. "It depends on what kind of Calaspian she was. You may have inherited some of those traits." Traits that could explain her current condition. "What else do you know?"

"People had said she was attacked by a sea monster. There were stories of sightings at that lake. When she appeared out of nowhere, everyone assumed the two things were connected. To this day, no one in my family likes large bodies of water. We won't even swim in pools. And I've tried. Lots of people suggested it to help my breathing problems, since the rain helps me so much. But I couldn't bring myself to try."

"You have problems with your breathing?" Eric's eyes widened. He scanned her pale, dry skin and cracked lips. Finally, everything was starting to make sense.

"Sometimes. It's actually been getting bad again, since I've been out in all this sand." She massaged her chest lightly, struggling to take in a deep breath. "The air is so dry."

"That makes sense."

"How's that?" Wheels turned, but she couldn't put the pieces together.

"Your ancestor was the sea monster," he revealed. "She must have spent time at that lake in animal form, before she fell. Your need to be around water is exactly how a Calaspian with a water affinity reacts when they spend too much time out of water. The way your body is responding to being in this desert versus how you were on Earth, in the rain... it all lines up. Even your family's fear of swimming fits. Fallen often feel a fear of things that remind them of where they came from. That can be passed down to descendants. In most instances, that's all that's inherited, but in some cases, like yours, the animal spirit itself can be passed down." A half laugh, half sigh revealed his relief. This he could understand. This, he knew how to fix. Once she was around water again, she'd be fine; her body would regenerate and heal.

"So, you're saying, that I spent the better part of twenty years going to doctors for something that would have been fine if I'd just learned to swim and spent more time in the water?" she asked incredulously, swallowing hard.

Eric's relief faltered. "Yes." Twenty years? She'd suffered most of her life over something she'd not needed to. If only he could have found her sooner—how much pain he could have saved her.

With a laughing, half sob, she lay her head back and sighed. "That sounds about right. What about the rest of my family? Do they have this animal spirit inside them, too?"

"If they don't share your breathing affliction, I'd say no. They most likely just inherited the residual fear of water."

She was quiet for a long while, but he could feel her mind swirling with thoughts. He could only imagine what it must be like to process this news. Even learning of Calaspia hadn't challenged her self-identity this way. This meant looking at memories in an entirely new way; it rewrote her history, as well as her family's. "She was an eel," Nancy said at last, looking at the pendant.

"How do you know?" he asked, curiously.

"The sea monster was always described as being serpentine in shape, like a giant eel. And the pendant," she added, staring at it, "has this cut on it. Everyone always said it was just a scratch, damage from the attack, but I'd always thought it kind of looked like an eel."

Taking the stone, he studied the mark. "It does," he agreed, "and carving our totem animal onto one's pendant is a common practice—wait a second. There was this woman, an eel demonic, I think, who fell a couple hundred years ago, after her brother was murdered."

"Two hundred years?" She considered it. "The timing sounds right. What happened?"

"There was a panther angelic obsessed with her. He became angry and killed her brother. She fell and the panther was banished. There were some secondary falls from those who couldn't accept what had happened. It was worse with the land and water affinities who knew them. Those who were of an avian nature stayed mainly to ourselves, but it had been a pretty big deal."

"Which would make this banished man in the desert the one who'd caused the fall of Adeline, who I apparently look a lot like, so much so he initially thought I was her."

He felt her heart clench with fear. "We're together, and once we get back to Calaspia and back to regular time, he won't be able to harm you."

She was still worried about having a murderous, mad man obsessed with her likeness prowl out there, but Eric's words and presence did wonders to ease her fears. "This explains so much, but does this mean I've never been human?" She couldn't contain the pain and confusion in her question.

Clasping the hand that held the bird, Eric smiled soothingly. "You're more human than I am. My mother had already bonded with the hawk before I was conceived. Unless your other parent is also harboring a latent fallen Calaspian in their lineage, you're presumably at least half human. Even at that, your Calaspian ties aren't fully undiluted. Add to that your human upbringing, and I'd say your human side and nature are strong. You're human. You're just also something more."

"Yay," she responded sarcastically. A sad bitterness zipped through their connection.

"How bad was it?" He was afraid of the answer.

She stared forward. "I've spent hundreds of nights curled up in bed, gasping for air, my chest burning. There were so many things I didn't do, places I didn't go, because I was afraid of having an attack. I lost jobs and apartments, missed entire semesters at school. Cindy," her voice choked with tears, "took me in, offered to pay bills and take care of whatever else I needed. She got me a part-time job at her work to help me with doctor bills. She's my little sister, and she was the one who had to take care of me. I was helpless and useless, and a complete burden on everyone around me. To think the solution was so simple ..." She turned to him. "Are you sure? Are you *really* sure about this? I need to know if this is for real."

Her desperate need to know surged through him. Leaning close, he shut his eyes and transmitted his mind to hers, which was completely open to him. She held nothing back. Her pain, trust, and need were as strong as if they belonged to him. Pushing further, to the innermost reaches of her mind and soul, he located that spark of life force, that essence that made Nancy who she was. Near her nexus, he found the vortex of swirling energy that signaled their burgeoning connection, and beside it he experienced another vortex of power all on its own. Blinding in its intensity, it had the strength of a full Calaspian, an eel, just as she'd sensed it.

He met her pleading gaze. "I'm sure." Relief softened her face and he dropped his gaze to the hand clutched to her chest. A hint of the tightness within her stirred in his own chest. Eric wanted to ease her pain, but what could he do? At home, he could take her to water. Here ... here she'd continue to suffer.

"It's not that bad as long as I stay calm." Pain-filled eyes belied her words. Her eel spirit couldn't survive this desert.

Without preamble, he kissed her. Gentle but demanding, he poured all of his feelings for her into the kiss, calling to the hawk within her, waiting until he was sure of the response, and not allowing the kiss to end until the pressure left his chest.

She reeled in surprise and swayed in his arms. Her head lay against his as she drew several shaky breaths. "We may have a different definition for calm," she joked, her voice nearly normal.

Eric chuckled, enjoying the feel of her hair against his skin. It felt fuller and healthier. Pulling back, he could see her complexion was also much better. Color was back in her cheeks and her lips were no longer dry. "How's your breathing?"

She took a deep breath and sat straighter. She stretched an arm and flexed her hand, noticing increased energy and strength. "How did you do that?"

"Calaspians with a dual affinity generally have one or the other in greater control at any given time. I simply encouraged the hawk within you closer to the surface."

"Which pushed the eel back," she added. He nodded. "So, you're saying if I let you kiss me, I'll never have problems breathing again?" She arched an eyebrow and grinned.

"Maybe not 'never', but I'm willing to give it a try, if that's what you want." His kiss was soft and delicate. Both smiled contentedly as their noses playfully touched.

"Very selfless," she nodded sagely, looking more like she had when they'd met. Even the cuts on her face and arms were beginning to fade.

"I live to serve," he joked. And then he saw her eyes— bright yellow irises and specks of red and brown. Hawk eyes. "So beautiful," he murmured.

Her brows knitted in confusion. "What is it?"

"You have hawk eyes, my dear."

"Hawk eyes?" She looked around, noticing changes to her vision. "So many colors," she said, awestruck. "I don't even know what most of them are called." She glanced at the bird figure in her hand. "All this detail." Gazing upward, she ran a hand along his cheek, as though seeing him for the first time. Giddy, her aura pulsed with excitement. Then, her eyes changed back to human. She blinked. "I never realized how much of your vision you sacrifice when you take human eyes. I'm so sorry I ever asked you to do that."

"I'll gladly take whatever form you ask. They're both part of me, just as you're part of me."

"Change your eyes."

He complied with a quick blink. "Do they still make you nervous?"

She regarded him closely, considering her response. She still couldn't exactly tell where he was looking. "I ... I'm not sure anymore."

He blinked again and his eyes returned to human. "Let me know when you are. Until then, I'll gladly look at you with these." Staring deeply into her eyes, he repeated his compliment. "So beautiful."

"But they're human again."

"And no less beautiful." Gently, he pushed hair from her face.

Nancy leaned into the touch, no longer trying to hide her reaction. She felt the stirrings of something new within. Ever since the kiss and the eye transformation, she felt different. Was this the hawk spirit he'd spoken of? It didn't feel like having an alien spirit inhabiting her body. It felt natural, like another part of herself. And he'd said she had an eel spirit, too. A dual affinity, that was what he called it. With so many other spirits inside, where did that leave the human side? Hawks were air creatures. Eels were water. She was most comfortable with her feet firmly on the ground. Would the animal elements take over?

Would she lose who she was? "Are there a lot of dual affinities?"

"There are some, but not many. Most matings occur within the same animal, or at least within the same realm of earth, air, or water. There aren't many crossovers."

"Like me?"

"Like you," he agreed.

"Is that why Adeline rejected the panther? He wasn't her kind."

He took a deep breath, sensing the question behind the question. "Perhaps. Those who pursue a mate outside of a divine matching rarely go outside their specific animal affinity, but matings like ours are very different. We were brought together because you're my perfect mate, and I'm yours. Nothing else matters. I'd give my life to protect you."

She blushed, but smiled wryly. "You'd give your life to protect anyone. That's the kind of person you are."

Eric cupped her face, his gaze pointed. "You're precious to me."

"I know," she responded truthfully. She could feel that easily enough. His feelings for her were very real. She laid her head back on his chest and hugged him tightly. And so they sat, holding each other appreciatively.

CHAPTER ELEVEN

Ephraim drifted in and out of consciousness. He was aware of gentle hands moving across his body, expertly setting broken bones and bandaging injuries. She talked as she worked. He couldn't follow the words, and he didn't understand much of what he heard, but her voice was soothing.

When he finally awakened, his head felt much clearer. The young woman was sitting nearby, on the floor, her back against a wall. She was fast asleep. Her clothes and skin were covered in dried blood. His. The room was strange, unlike any he knew. Where was he? It wasn't Calaspia. Of that much, he was sure. He extended his senses. Could this be Earth? Had Solstice magic brought him to Earth?

Ephraim sat up quietly, but she woke immediately. "Be careful moving. How are you feeling?"

She scooted over and began reexamining his wounds. "How did you get so beat up?" she asked without waiting for an answer to the earlier question. Clasping his face, she shone a small light in each eye. Seemingly satisfied, she then checked his leg. "Can you move this? I don't think it's broken, but without an x-ray, I can't know for sure. I bound it as tightly as I could. You'll want to be careful for a while, just in case." Ephraim chuckled, and she looked up, surprised. "I'm doing it again, aren't I? I'm sorry. My patients can't usually talk, so I get carried away sometimes. How are you feeling?" she repeated.

"Much better. Thank you." Ephraim studied the intense light-blue eyes and furrowed forehead framed by glossy black curls. She took his breath away. If he'd had any doubt about seeing Solstice magic before he passed out, it was now gone. This woman was most definitely his mate. Despite the pain, he could think of little but his desire for her.

"How did you get injured?" She went back to checking the bandages and testing his arm for range of motion and level of pain.

"I fell," her eyebrows arched as he quietly explained, "from a substantial height ... onto jagged rocks."

"Yeah," she nodded. "That would fit the injuries, all right. Okay, so next question, and please don't take this the wrong way, but *what* are you? These wings are fantastic. Can you really fly with them?" She touched the soft feathers appreciatively. "I'm sorry. Is that rude? I should have asked before touching them."

He laughed. "After everything you've done for me?" he asked, incredulous. "You're not rude," he assured her. "And yes, I can fly, or at least I'll be able to again, soon."

"Oh, I wouldn't recommend using this wing for a least a couple of weeks."

"My kind heal quickly," he informed her.

"And what is your kind?"

"I'm from a place called Calaspia."

"And there are others like you?" she asked excitedly.

"Well, none are *exactly* like me," he winked, feeling more like his old self.

She grinned and tucked a curl behind her ear, suddenly noticing what she looked like. "Well, the immediate danger seems to have passed, and I'm a mess. I should clean up. And super healing or not, you should rest. Some injuries were pretty bad. There were moments ..." her voice trailed off and she patted his hand. "Seriously, you should rest. There are water bottles and fruit on the counter. I'll be back in a few minutes. Make yourself at home."

Picking up bandages and supplies, she disappeared quickly behind a door.

———

ERIC SIGHED CONTENTEDLY and held Nancy close. This moment would be perfect if they weren't lost in the sands of time, with no apparent way home, his brother injured and waiting for him to return and bring a healer. Ephraim. He stretched his senses to get an indication of his current condition, and sat up in surprise.

Nancy regarded him curiously. Then, her eyes widened with understanding. "Your brother?"

"He isn't on Calaspia. He's on Earth. I ... I can't get a good read, but I'm sure that's where he is."

"Is it the Solstice magic?" she asked.

"I think so," he laughed.

"So, does that mean he has an Earth mate, too?"

Eric nodded. "That's the only conclusion that makes sense." His mother was right after all. They'd both found mates this year. Greater powers were at work, weaving everything together exactly the way it was always meant to happen. Ephraim would be okay. With that worry off his back, Eric wrapped Nancy tightly in his arms and leaned back against the boat.

Nancy's joy mingled with his, buoying each other's contentment. Eric inhaled her scent, enjoying the feel of her arms around him. His Nancy. His mate. Eric grinned boyishly.

"What?" she asked suspiciously.

"You said, 'too'."

"Too?"

"You said, 'he has an Earth mate, too'. That's the first time you've referred to yourself, even indirectly, as my mate."

Nancy looked away in thought. "I guess it is." She looked back.

Eric brushed hair from her face and spoke softly. "And how do you feel about that?"

"Hmmm." She curled a hand over his and inhaled deeply. "Like maybe it wouldn't be the worst thing in the world ... worlds ... dimensions." She chuckled softly and hugged him again, resting a cheek against his chest. "And how do you feel about me being ... part ... eel? That feels so weird to say out loud."

"One of my brothers is mated to a bobcat angelic." He shrugged.

"How does that work? Don't cats hunt birds?"

Startled, Eric choked back a cough. "Um ... yeah ... they uh ... they have figured out different ways ... to um, focus her ... instincts. Ways which my brother takes a great deal of joy in describing in meticulous detail."

Nancy's hand flew to her mouth. "Oh, my!"

"He always does it right before family dinners," Eric continued with a far off, tortured gaze. "Then, he makes obscure references throughout dinner, in front of our parents."

Nancy doubled over, laughing. "That's hilarious."

"I couldn't look his mate in the eye for an entire moon cycle."

Nancy's laughter exploded. She wiped tears from her eyes and sighed contentedly. Eric brushed aside the lock of hair that persistently fell into her face. His fingers lingered and their gazes locked.

The sounds of sand flying against the ship were soothing. They were still lost, far from home, with dangerous beasts and banished beings out there searching for them, but for the moment, they were alone and safe.

"How's your breathing?" he asked.

"My breathing?" Her nose crinkled with suspicion.

Her ability to read him was becoming increasingly impressive. He struggled to keep a straight face. "Do you require my assistance?"

A breath caught as her gaze dropped to his lips. "I'm good."

"Are you sure? You seem ... breathless."

"Yeah," she admitted, "but I don't think kissing will help in this case."

"Won't know unless we try." His grin widened.

"I'm beginning to feel a little thirsty," she admitted.

"Oh, well in that case." He pressed his lips to hers, holding her tenderly. A shiver rolled down her body. He felt her need and his own. "How was that?"

"Hmmm, nice, very nice, very *very* nice."

They laughed softly.

"But I'm still thirsty, and the air is unbearably dry. I think that little trick of yours may be wearing off, and I'm pretty much useless during a full-blown breathing attack."

Eric clasped her shoulder. "The wind sounds like it is dying down out there. We'll find water."

"How? We're in a desert."

He helped her up and pulled back the tarp, leading her outside. "There's supposed to be a town to the east. There should be a water source there."

"A town? How's there a town in the sands of time?"

"It was founded and settled by the people who have ever been—or will ever be—lost here."

"Will ever? You mean people from the future are here?"

"So they say. I've never actually been here before this, mind you. All I know is what I've heard from stories."

"How do they get here?" She scanned the vehicle grave-yard half buried in sand. "How do all these boats and planes, and everything else, get here?"

"Thin spots between worlds. When people and things accidentally find themselves in those spots, some of them disappear from their world and appear here."

"You mean like the portals between Earth and Calaspia?" She dragged her feet across the thick heavy sand as the bright sun beat down. What she wouldn't give for a nice, cool rainstorm right now.

"They are very similar, yes. Someone in the city may know of a portal to Calaspia from here. At the very least, it should give us a place to regroup, and there should be water."

"Okay," she said uncertainly. There should be water. What if there *wasn't*? Nancy paused, considering words, and then spoke. "You mentioned people used to travel between worlds without portals."

Eric took a deep breath and let it out. The thought of traveling without portals terrified him. "That was when the connection between the worlds was stronger, and not everyone could do it. It's ... tricky. A wrong move, and you could end up ..."

"Lost in the sands of time?" she finished for him.

He shrugged. "You have a point, but still, I've never done it. I've never known anyone who has done it. World jumping isn't a skill everyone has."

"What if it's not a skill?" she asked, suddenly excited. She gaped, seeing everything and nothing. The wheels in her mind were turning. She felt she was on the verge of understanding something. "What if it's about willpower and faith? You just have to *will* yourself to be where you need to be, and have faith it *will* work."

Eric looked at her closely, considering what she'd said, and feeling her confidence. "Alright." He shut his eyes and she felt energy gather around them. She sensed his intense concentration and desire to go home, perceived his hesitation and uncertainly. He was trying this for her, because she believed it would work, yet he didn't fully believe he could do it. He wasn't certain it would work. The gathering energy dissipated and he opened his eyes. "Nothing," he said quietly.

He hadn't felt how close he was. How had she felt it? It seemed obvious to her. She felt she could do it, only she didn't know where she was going. She'd never been to Calaspia. That felt important, somehow. He could get them there; she knew he could. He just had to *believe* it. As long as he doubted, it wouldn't work. He was capable of more than he knew. She recognized this as an absolute certainty. Her heartbeat quickened with excitement and her skin prickled. Hairs stood on end. She felt connected to something bigger than herself.

Her vision grew dark, and she felt herself falling and gasping for air. As her vision cleared, she saw Eric above her, concerned, stroking her hair. The sense of connection was gone. Her entire mind was focused on breathing. Her mind swam. Years of practice allowed for her to pursue visualizations to calm the body. Only ... they didn't work this time. Concern from Eric washed over her.

"No," she told herself. This was nothing new. She'd had breathing attacks before. It would end. Calm. Breathe. Calm. Breathe. But with Eric's panic merging with her own, that was easier said than done.

Realization was visible in Eric's eyes. His breathing slowed as calming emotions flowed through their connection. With a loud gasp of relief, she rode the crest and her breathing returned to normal. Her chest and head ached, but she was used to that. This, too, would subside. She rested her forehead against his shoulder and breathed slowly. Her fingers rested lightly on his arms.

Where had that attack come from? They usually started out gradually and grew stronger over time. Was it because Eric had stopped the attack from happening in the boat? Or did it have something to do with her earlier train of thought? She was overwhelmed with certainty and insight. Maybe she was tapping into that Calaspian part of her. Had she inadvertently called the eel part of her to the surface? She loved the feeling of connection, but did she dare pursue it? Until she figured that out, she needed to be careful—or at least until she was near water.

"I told you I was useless during a breathing attack," she joked with a half grin.

"This ... is normal for you?" He sounded shocked.

"More or less. They aren't usually this sudden, but yeah, this is normal." She felt his arms tighten protectively. "It's alright. Until today, I've never understood why this was happening. You have no idea what a relief it is to finally have answers." She hugged him tightly and felt tears trickle down her cheeks.

Gently, he stroked her head. The wind kicked up sand, but his wings were around them in an instant, blocking sand and sun. She wanted to kiss him, but she was nervous. Sure, they'd kissed before, but he'd initiated the contact those times. She laughed to herself. How stupid was that? She'd faced phantom beasts, breathing attacks, and being lost in the sands of time, but the thought of kissing a handsome, kind and strong man who cared for her and protected her made her nervous. She rubbed her cheek against his neck and face, then stopped so that their cheeks touched. Her heart raced with anticipation.

Eric drew a sharp breath, but remained still, waiting for her to make the next move. Gathering courage, she quickly kissed his cheek and tucked her face back into his chest. Eric remained still a few more seconds, then released a small chuckle and hugged her tightly.

Resting his chin on her head, he held her close. Her embarrassment disappeared, replaced by frustration. What was wrong with her? She didn't want a chaste peck on the cheek. She wanted an intense, lingering kiss. She knew how he felt about her. Before she could second-guess her actions and chicken out again, Nancy sat up and kissed Eric fully on the lips. It was demanding, nervous, excited, scared, passionate, hesitant ... and utterly right.

Eric released her arms. His body shook with need, but he allowed her to set the pace and boundaries. When she pulled back, body shaking from nerves and excitement, he didn't push further contact. They sat, breathing heavily, heads touching.

She wanted to kiss him again. She almost did just that, but she knew what would happen if she did. Her body cried out for his, feeling his need as clearly as her own. His level of restraint was incredible, but not resolute. If she pushed it now, he wouldn't stop at a kiss, and she wouldn't stop him, either. Already her body wanted her to cease overthinking everything and do what she knew they both wanted. Her brain won. Sitting back, a field of energy stretched between them, pulling her toward him. She resisted the pull. "How far do you think this city is?" Her voice sounded hoarse and raspy, but she accepted speech as success and ignored it.

"I don't know," he answered, "but we'll find it faster flying than walking."

She whimpered ... an actual whimper, like that of a puppy or child. "Okay," she answered shakily. She couldn't argue with logic, as much as she wanted to, and she really, really, really, *really* wanted to.

"What is it about heights that frightens you so?"

"Being so far from the ground," she answered easily. "I look down, and suddenly my head is spinning. I feel like my body belongs to someone else. Nothing feels right, like I'm floating outside my head and don't actually control my legs and arms. Or I do, but the connection is sluggish, like when you try to walk when your foot has fallen asleep. I feel like I'm going to start falling and won't be able to stop it. Then, all I can think about is the ground rushing up to meet me as I plummet to my death." Her voice trailed off dramatically and widened eyes stared off into the middle distance.

Eric laughed. "Wow! That was detailed." He rubbed his chin and neck thoughtfully. "Okay." Taking both of her hands, he looked deeply into her eyes and waited until he had her complete attention. "I've been flying since I was a child. No matter how long you fly, there's always a little risk of falling. There's risk with anything you do, but to fly is an incredible gift. You get to see the world in a way most people never do. Flying is freedom."

"Maybe for you, but I don't have wings. If I fall, I fall. I can't stop. I broke two bones falling from a tree when I was a kid, and that was only five feet. Granted, that tree I climbed to hide in before you found me here in the desert was taller than that, but I still fell out of it, and that wasn't as high as flying in the sky. That's waaaayyyy higher."

"You climbed a tree?" he asked proudly.

"Don't get so excited. I was terrible at it. Did you not hear the part about falling and breaking bones?

"As long as I'm with you in the sky, I won't let you fall. You have my word. I'll protect you, no matter what. Besides," he smirked, "If you do fall, you should heal much faster now."

She rolled her eyes. "I'm still afraid," she admitted reluctantly. "I believe you. I trust you, but I'm still afraid. I don't want to be afraid. I'm tired of being afraid." She met Eric's understanding gaze.

"Focus on me and focus on the beauty of the world around you. There won't be any room left for fear. When you focus on the good things around you, the bad things have no power."

"Okay," she sighed. "I'll try." Her expression conveyed nervousness. She let Eric help her to her feet and stepped into his arms. Hugging him tightly, she tried to release her nervous energy. She was only a little less than moderately successful. When she looked up, she saw he was in complete hawk form, down to his eyes. She cupped his cheek and studied him closely. After what felt like minutes, she spoke. "They don't make me nervous anymore." She meant it. Those hawk eyes were part of him.

He let out the breath he'd been holding and kissed her;

she felt elation and hope swell inside of him. And then, they were airborne. Still kissing her deeply, he took them high into the sky. When the kiss ended, and she could again look around, her first impulse was to cling tightly with fear. He wouldn't let her go, she reminded herself. She was safe. He'd protect her. Letting out an anxious breath, she turned to peer around. Ignoring the height and fear, she regarded miles of sand dunes and a stunning, glistening sun. There was light everywhere. How incredible would it be to explore the sand-covered vessels scattered below and solve centuries of mysteries. The answers were right below.

"I see something over there." Eric was staring into the eastern horizon. "It's a good distance away, but it could be the city. Are you good to fly it?"

See the beauty, she reminded herself. Focus on Eric. Nodding, she hugged him more tightly and concentrated on the feel of his arms around her. Eric took off like a bullet. Remembering how dizzying their flight here had been, she closed her eyes and thought only of Eric, focusing on the feel of his feathers and beating heart.

Focus on Eric, she repeated every time her mind wandered. Focus on Eric. The words became a silent chant. She thought about the feel of his skin, the color of his feathers, the places his body transitioned from skin to feathers; she immersed herself in how everything felt. She considered the flexing of his powerful back muscles surrounding the base of his majestic wings. Not for the first time, she imagined those muscles flexing for another reason. Her body grew hot, and she felt Eric's react in response. Visions of him filled her mind. When she opened her eyes, she viewed a world filled with brilliant color and crystal-sharp details.

The once blurry muddle of browns and grays flying by down below was now bright and rich, and beautiful. Her eyes had changed. She lost herself in the multitude of colors on Eric's chest and imagined them pressed against her bare skin. Eric wobbled for a second and, catching himself, straightened his flight trajectory. Her thoughts were affecting him. *She* was affecting him. But she couldn't seem to stop. Those mated felt an uncontrollable attraction to each another. That was what he'd told her. She felt the attraction and their steadfast connection. The thought of being supernaturally mated across time and space no longer seemed crazy. It felt real and right.

Their feet touched the ground and Eric pressed her against a flat stone wall. Before she could fully register that they'd landed, Eric grabbed her head and ravaged her mouth with his. Pressing his body against hers, she knew there'd be no holding back. Consumed by his arousal and overwhelmed by her innumerable passionate thoughts during the flight, he was no longer acting on anything but instinct. She'd brought him to this state, and she was about to enjoy every second of the consequence.

Eric's eager lips ran down her neck and chest. His hands roamed her body, clutching and fondling. She was his to possess, and in the moment, she was more than fine with that.

A horn blared. They ignored it, unconcerned with the rest of the world. It blared again, then a third time. "Take shelter!" a voice shouted. "Time storm approaching!"

Breathing heavily, Eric reluctantly retreated a step. Nancy nearly sank on legs feeling of gelatin, but she managed to stumble along with him, hand in hand, and they trekked around the building. She looked around. Her eyes were human again. Eric had changed to his human form beside her. They watched the chaos—dozens of people rushing around the streets, running into buildings, slamming doors, and bolting windows. The wind was picking up, but it was actually quite pleasant and cool.

"Are you deaf? Take shelter," a woman said from beside. Something in the confused look on Nancy's face must have given them away, because the woman grabbed Nancy's free hand and pulled them into the building they'd been making out against. She secured the door. She then, hurriedly, worked on the windows. When she was done, she turned. "New to Allegretarde?" she asked, then nodded, answering her own question. "You're lucky you came together. Most people show up alone. Have a seat. The storm will take a while. Do you need anything?"

Thunder shook the small building and the sound of rain pounding the roof called to Nancy. She looked longingly at the door, wanting desperately to go outside. Idly, she rubbed her chest.

"Do you have any water?" Eric asked.

Nancy barely heard him or noticed what he was doing until he pressed a cool glass into her hands. She gulped it quickly. It wasn't as refreshing as feeling water on her skin, but it did help. Eric handed her a second glass and she sucked that one down, too. He handed the empty glasses back to the woman with a grateful smile.

She looked down and whistled. "Dang. Been out in the sands a while, I take it." Without asking, she refilled them and handed them back.

This time, Nancy let Eric keep one and drank her water at a more leisurely pace.

Nancy took in the surroundings—a sitting room, dining room, kitchen. Two doors exited off the main room. The place was small, but not uncomfortable. Their host was a woman who looked to be in her twenties. She had a tell-tell rounded belly and lowered herself heavily into a plush armchair.

Eric walked up behind Nancy and put a hand on her shoulder. Casually, he massaged the tension from her shoulders and neck.

One of the two doors opened and a young girl came running out. "Why didn't you wake me? I told you this was the storm." She ran to the front door and pulled free the latch.

"Mom!" the woman yelled. "What if you're wrong? You can't go out there." She hurriedly stood and hastened to the door.

The girl gave a stern look. "I've charted the storms for a year. This one will work. I'm not staying in this child's body forever. Move aside!"

With a resigned sigh, the young woman moved aside and allowed the girl to open the door. The moment she was clear, the woman closed the door behind her and returned to the chair.

"What's the deal with these storms?" Nancy asked.

"They're time storms," she answered simply. "They charge the air outside and speed up or slow down time wherever they travel, especially anywhere the lightning strikes."

"So ... that girl?"

"Is my mom. She got caught in a storm years ago and began aging in reverse. She's been obsessed with the storms ever since, trying to find one that will switch her back. The only problem is that time storms are unpredictable. Just when you think you understand them, they do something completely unexpected. They can easily kill you in hundreds of different ways."

Nancy thought back to the lightning in the desert. Was

that from a time storm? She'd been out there, without shelter. A memory flashed of her being high in the storm clouds, dodging lightning, and she felt her heart lodge in her throat. She glanced at Eric, realizing again what he'd gone through to get to her.

"Thank you for allowing us to shelter in your home," Eric said graciously. Stepping around the couch, he sat beside Nancy and put a protective hand on her leg.

"My mom was a child when she came here. She never would have survived without the help of those here. We try not to forget that."

"How far along are you?" Nancy asked.

"Four years," the woman answered with a smile, patting her belly. "Only one more year to go, so I'm in the home stretch."

Nancy felt her eyes widen, but wasn't sure what to say. A five-year pregnancy?

The woman smiled again. "I've heard pregnancies go quite a bit faster in the other worlds. Things move at their own pace here," she explained. "Sometimes we wake up, and the town is new, freshly built. Other times, it's falling down around us. Occasionally, we wake up to an empty desert and have to start from scratch, only to find it full the next day. While our individual lives move in the regular way, baring time storms of course, the world around us doesn't move in a linear pattern. Stay here long enough and you'll understand."

"Do you know if there are any Calaspian or Earth portals around here?" Eric leaned forward on his elbows.

"If there are, they move around. No one who has ever come here has been able to return the same way. The rifts don't stay in one place long enough. Supposedly, there's a pattern to the changes, as with the storms, but tracking them is no easy task, and mistakes are easy to make. You have to be able to place each new day into an ordinal time line to see the changes, and most days bear very little difference to the next. While it's easy to see when we wake up in a time before the city, versus after or during when it was built, any time after its completion blends in to the next. You might notice a door painted a new color or see a missing garden, but even this can be obscured by the time storms. And even if you could somehow figure out what day you're in, you'd still have to find the rifts again each day, which is nearly impossible to do. I'm sorry."

"So, no one can leave here?" Anxious, Nancy was now sitting forward, too.

"Oh, people leave. Some walk off into the sands. No telling what happens to them, or what they find. Others disappear in a time storm or wander off and never come back. It's impossible to know if they found a way home or went somewhere else. But it *is* possible to leave."

Nancy saw Eric's features express disappointment. She was struck again with the knowledge that they didn't need to find a portal. Eric was the key to getting them home. Nancy gave a start. When had she begun to think of Calaspia as home? She'd never been there. She hadn't even completed the mating, no matter how close they'd gotten. Dizziness swelled and once again she wished to go out into the storm. "Is there water around here? A lake? A river? Big fountains?"

"Sorry, but all the water comes from underground wells. It's enough to live off, but I'm afraid there's not much more than that."

The front door slammed open. A young woman stood defiantly in the threshold. "I told you it would work!" Outside, the sounds of the storm were lessening.

"Mom?" Their host walked toward the door. She smiled and hugged the woman. "Please tell me you're done going out in storms."

"Probably."

"Probably? Mother, don't you dare go back out there. You could end up a baby next time, and I'm not taking care of two babies at once."

The woman shrugged limply and headed to the door she'd exited earlier. Her daughter followed, house guests forgotten. The door closed behind, so whatever reply her mother gave was lost.

A siren sounded outside, and they could hear people moving around the streets. Nancy hurried to the door and raced outside, searching for pooled water from the rain. A few muddy puddles were already drying. A drop of orange rainwater fell from the eaves of the porch onto her foot and was instantly absorbed into her skin. She needed more. So much more. How could she have never realized it? It seemed so obvious now. The thirst. The dry skin. She felt tired and weak, old and dehydrated. How had she only noticed the pain of breathing? This was so much more than that. And where were her sneakers? She wriggled her toes in the sand and realized she had no idea where she'd last seen them. She was just as oblivious about her unique needs now as she had been all these years.

But she hadn't been that oblivious, she reminded herself. She'd noticed the need for water, if only superficially. She knew baths helped. How was she supposed to know what was wrong with her? She never knew about animal spirits and other dimensional worlds. Still, she should have tried swimming. She should have pushed past the fears and done what she knew needed to be done, and what she knew needed to be done now.

Nancy felt Eric behind, standing quietly at the door. He came forward and put a hand on her shoulder. It was a simple touch, but their combined emotions flowed through it. He was concerned for her. She didn't blame him. There weren't any mirrors, but she could imagine how bad her appearance was. She felt terrible and he could feel that, too.

"I'm going to take a quick flight around the city. Maybe I'll be able to pick up a sense of a portal or see some water."

"She said there wasn't any."

"You never know. With the rain, maybe some collected somewhere. It won't hurt to check. Stay here. I'll be back."

"The beasts?" she asked, reluctant to be separated.

"They shouldn't attack in the city. Just stay around people. I'll be right back. I won't be long. I promise." Seeing her sad expression, he leaned forward and kissed her.

She let her lips linger on his. His feelings were even stronger now that they were touching in such an intimate way. He was overwhelmed, carrying the weight of two worlds on his shoulders. She felt his burden and concerns. "Fly," she whispered.

Eric transformed, kissed her again, and took flight.

CHAPTER TWELVE

The city was in an odd state of flux, likely the aftereffects of the time storm. Buildings alternated between appearing new and dilapidated. Trees that were saplings when they approached were now massive giants. Grass shriveled and turned to brown, then sprouted tall and green. Leaves changed from green to orange, and fell to the ground. A minute later, the trees were full of leaves again. Streets that had been clean and clear were overgrown with vines. Random animal bones lay where some unfortunate creatures had failed to find shelter from the storm. The only water was an occasional puddle, nothing substantial, and he could not get a sense of any nearby portal energy. It was just as the woman had said. They'd have to find another way.

Turning around, he flew back to the house.

———

HE COULDN'T GET her face out of his mind. After an eternity of fragile half thoughts and memories, this one was crystal clear. Her clothes were strange, and her hair was different. He could have sworn she had a cluster of freckles by her left eye, along her cheekbone, but that must have been wrong, along with the thoughts that her nose wasn't always so sharply upturned. It was her. It *had* to be her. The eyes ... no one else could have those eyes. Besides, he could sense the eel spirit in her. She didn't appear to remember him, but that didn't matter. Memories could be lost. He knew that all too well.

Adeline. Seeing her again brought back images of the first time they'd met. He'd hurt his paw taking a jump and landing the wrong way on rocks he'd not seen. Coming to the water to rest and recover, she'd emerged from the lake. Water glistening like jewels on her scales, those piercing ice-blue eyes, he'd loved her instantly. Touching her hands to his injured foot, he felt her healing ease the pain. With a pretty smile, she bid him well and jumped back in the water.

Gelick took a deep breath. That had been the most complete memory he could recall in a very long time. He stared in shock. How could he have forgotten his sweet Adeline? He must find her again. Tiny shadows darted along the horizon. They were avoiding him. On the ground lay the fading corpses of several beasts, the unlucky few to feel the full brunt of his anger. They'd let her escape. They'd let that hawk take her.

One of the beasts whimpered and crawled forward slowly, carrying something in its mouth. He dropped the items at Gelick's feet and quickly jumped back, waiting for a reaction. Gelick squatted to the ground and looked at the pink and black shoes. They were well worn, with laces matted together by dried dirt. The soles showed impressions where her feet had been, and the bottoms were slick. He picked up the shoes, *her* shoes, and turned them over.

"Is this some kind of joke?" The beast took a step back. "I told you to find the girl, and instead you bring me shoes!" He threw them and slowed time, appearing beside the beast before it could escape. Grabbing it around the neck, he sucked its life energy until it was empty, then tossed the body over by the others.

"Come!" he commanded. The other phantoms ran forward to obey, afraid of angering him further.

"How hard can it be to find one woman? You'll find her and destroy that hawk who's keeping her from me. Just like your brother, Adeline. Why are people always keeping us apart? You know we belong together." The phantoms scrabbled in confusion. He ignored them. His Adeline was back and nothing else mattered.

A howling beast ran from the east. It stopped beside Gelick and lowered its head submissively. He grabbed it and began pulling energy, tapping into the beast's memories. He saw the outer edges of the city landscape. A man with hawk wings flew above it. Gelick let go of the beast and it slunk into the crowd of other phantoms. "They're at the city."

The beasts grumbled and whimpered. None of them wanted to go there, not when they could sense much easier prey elsewhere.

"Go to the city," he commanded. "Find them. Bring her to me, and kill that hawk."

The beasts darted off to obey.

———

"YOU KNOW," Cindy said, coming out the bedroom with a towel covering wet hair, and fuzzy rabbit slippers on her feet, "I realized you were pretty much unconscious when we exchanged names, so you may not remember, but my name is Cindy."

"Ephraim," her mystery patient responded from where he stood by the mantle, looking at family pictures.

She walked up behind him and began checking his injuries again. "You're right about being a fast healer. Just the fact that you can stand on that leg is impressive. These wounds are looking much better."

Ephraim allowed the examination with a patient smile. "You seem proficient at tending injuries."

"I'm an animal doctor," she answered nonchalantly, checking his eyes for signs of a concussion. He seemed to be in remarkable good health. She wouldn't have believed it possible if she hadn't treated the injuries herself.

"Really? That's good to know." He had that mischievous smirk.

"Why?" she grinned and put down her pocket flashlight. "Do you have regular need of medical assistance? Perhaps you make it a habit to fall from substantial heights onto jagged rocks?"

Ephraim laughed. "You never know."

Fear stabbed her when she thought of him getting hurt again. "Please, don't," she said. "I know you heal quickly, but you really shouldn't be taking unnecessary risks. You were in bad shape when you got here." She thought back to those first few hours. "You stopped breathing twice, and the blood loss ..."

She touched the large bandage on his side. "You had a gaping hole here. I thought I'd never get the bleeding to stop. You went through four bandages and some rough field stitches before it finally stopped. From the bits of rock and dirt I found, I'd say you can thank those rocks for that injury. And before that healing of yours kicked in, I was ninety percent sure you had a concussion. There were several times I was sure you weren't going to make it." Allowing those fears to be spoken aloud, she couldn't stop her body from shaking.

Ephraim stood still, shocked. "I'm sorry I frightened you. I'm grateful for everything you did. And I'm thankful I was brought to you when I was."

"How were you brought here?"

"Would you believe magic?"

Cindy laughed. "I'd probably believe just about anything, right now."

He grinned and took her hands. "There are portals between our worlds, but they aren't open most of the time. I believe it was the Solstice magic that brought me to your world."

"Solstice?"

"It's a time my people find their one true mate. The magic brings us together."

Her eyes widened. "So, your ... mate ... is on Earth?"

He leaned in, his eyes staring into hers. "Yes, without a doubt."

Cindy felt her heartbeat quicken. "How will you find her? Earth is a big place."

"That won't be a problem."

Cindy took a step back, knocking into the coffee table and tipping over a glass of water. Absently, she grabbed a washcloth and began cleaning the mess, careful to keep her back to Ephraim. His eyes ... they did something to her. She felt drawn to them.

Ephraim chuckled lightly and turned back to the fireplace. "Are these pictures of your family?" he asked.

"Uh, yeah," she said, looking over her shoulder. "Most are me and my sister, Nancy."

"This is Nancy?" he said, pointing.

Cindy walked over to where he was standing.

"Yep, that's her. She hates that picture, too." Cindy laughed, remembering the day she took it at the rock-climbing gym. Nancy had been so uncomfortable, but she did it, and Cindy got photographic proof of her climbing the wall, looking at her with a good-natured scowl. "I convinced her to go rock climbing to get her over her fear of heights."

"Did it work?"

"Not even close, but at least I got a good blackmail picture out of it. Every time she doesn't want to try some-thing, I remind her it can't be as bad as rock climbing. That usually does the trick. I have been able to get her to go on hikes, camping trips, and an extreme driving course."

"Ah, so you're the risk-taker in your family. I thought so."

Cindy blushed. "Yeah, okay. Nancy would probably agree with you on that assessment."

"So, that would mean you don't share your sister's fear of heights."

"Uh, no, I'm not afraid of heights. When I graduated high school, for my senior trip, I went hiking to the top of this really tall mountain and hang-glided down. Nancy told me I was crazy, but it was great. The view was fantastic. I'll never forget it."

A grin stretched across his face. "Good." He leaned close to her ear. "Because when this wing heals, I'm going to make love to you in the sky with clouds for pillows and the horizon for our bed."

She sucked in a breath. Her pulse quickened as images of what he'd described ran through her head. Ephraim's hand guided her face toward his. She opened her eyes to find his lips capturing hers. Her fingers explored his chest and back, avoiding the injuries. "This is crazy," she moaned as he kissed her neck.

"This is destiny," he answered back.

"You're injured," she argued weakly.

"Not that injured. Not where it counts. I had an excellent doctor patch me up." His eyes twinkled and her resistance crumbled. He pulled her to him and picked her up. A groan escaped.

Ephraim stepped forward and felt his leg give out. Pain shot through it and his side. His vision darkened and Cindy's arms were around him in an instant, supporting his weight and keeping him on his feet. Carefully, she led him to the couch and helped him sit.

She muttered a curse. "You're side is bleeding again. Hold on." Pulling back the bandage, she muttered again. "You pulled a stitch. I'm going to have to sew it closed again." She grimaced and looked at him apologetically.

Ephraim smiled charmingly, belying the pain in his eyes, and nodded. Cindy pulled out supplies and prepared to pierce his skin. Her hands paused, and she leaned forward to kiss Ephraim, catching him off guard. With a loving smile, she quickly and expertly sewed the stitches in quick motion, finishing before he could react. Then she captured his mouth in another kiss, holding it until he relaxed.

Ephraim sat in surprised silence as Cindy re-bandaged his side. When she finished, he touched her face gently, intent on kissing her passionately. He didn't get far. Both drew sharp breaths as his movement resulted in pain. Cindy looked at her side in shock. "I felt your pain." She gazed up in amazement.

"I'm greatly sorry. I never would have taken the risks I had if I'd known I'd be sharing this with you. I'll never do anything that stupid again." He shook his head and lowered it in shame.

Cindy laughed softly and touched his face. "It's okay."

"You aren't surprised or unnerved by the connection?"

Cindy grinned. "I guess that's weird, but everything right now is kind of weird, so I'm just going with it. Besides, feeling your pain will make it easier to keep an eye on your injuries. I'm just glad it didn't kick in until now. So, try not to bust anymore stitches."

Ephraim smiled wryly. "This could make it difficult to seduce you properly."

Cindy grinned and pushed him gently back on the couch. "Then, I guess you'll just have to get better first." Ephraim groaned and Cindy laughed. She unconsciously tucked hair behind her ear and nibbled her lip as she stood. "Get more rest, doctor's orders. And remember, I'll know if you push yourself too soon."

Ephraim groaned with frustration. "Why did I have to go flying in that cave?"

Cindy knelt on the floor and tweaked his nose playfully. "Cheer up. At the rate you're healing, you'll be good before you know it."

He took her hands in his. His eyes stared into hers. All pretenses dropped, leaving honest, raw emotion. The depth of his love and commitment to her was vast. Over a century of preparation had led to this moment. He felt complete and whole for the first time. Suddenly, life had meaning. He'd love and protect her forever.

Her bottom lip quivered, her eyes blinked, and her pulse quickened. Cindy drew a shaky breath. "Consider me properly seduced," she whispered.

They closed their eyes and pressed their foreheads together, swept away by the intensity of their emotions. He pressed his lips to hers as his hands caressed her back and head, his fingers weaving through her lustrous hair. She clasped his chest as she moved onto the couch and stretched out beside him. As Ephraim turned toward her, he experienced a sharp ache in his side.

Cindy cried out in surprise and pain.

"Urgghh," he grumbled.

Cindy laughed. "It's okay, Casanova. I'm sure you'll be back to your suave self soon." With a contented sigh, she lay her head on his chest and settled into his side.

Ephraim hugged her closely and closed his eyes. This may not be how he'd always envisioned this day going, but they were together, and that was all that mattered. He'd make it up to her later.

———

ERIC FLEW BACK to the house to find Nancy in the yard splashing herself with water from a dish on a pedestal. Landing, he looked around. There were tiny wooden houses and feeders full of seeds scattered around the yard. Eric laughed hard.

Nancy stopped splashing and looked at him quizzically. "What?"

Still laughing, he motioned the yard and then the pedestal. "That's a bird bath."

Nancy shot a stern look. She tried to hide a smile. Ignoring him, she turned back to the pedestal and tried to lift it. When that didn't work, she squatted down and tipped it over herself.

Still laughing, Eric walked over and helped her get the last of the water. He tilted the pedestal so it was straight and held out a hand to help her up. "There you go, my little bird." He no longer laughed, but his grin was wide.

Nancy shot another look, but accepted his help. "I'm never going to live this down, am I?"

He shook his head and his eyes gleamed with mirth. "Nope. I'm absolutely telling everyone I know, and probably some strangers."

Nancy rolled her eyes. "Awesome," she replied sarcastically.

Eric took her face in his hands and leaned forward, planting a kiss on the tip of her nose. "It's okay, my little bird." His voice was soft and comforting. "We only live forever."

Nancy groaned and rolled her eyes again. "How did your flight go?

He shook his head. "Nothing."

She looked hesitantly at him. "Eric, I know I said this before, but I don't think we need a portal."

Eric shifted uncomfortably. She felt his frustration. "I tried that."

"And it was working! I don't know why you couldn't sense it. I don't know why I could, but I did. I felt something happening. Then, I felt your doubt, and it all disappeared. It was there. You were so close, but you didn't think you could do it. But I *know* you can. It doesn't make any sense, but I'm positive I'm right."

His eyes narrowed. She felt his mind probing hers. "Why didn't you say this before?"

"I was about to, but then I couldn't breath, and ... I don't know. I thought maybe whatever I was feeling had somehow triggered the attack. I was afraid of it happening again before we neared water, but I guess the only way we'll get near now is if I *do* say something."

"How do you feel right now?"

"Like I'm slowly suffocating. The air ... it feels thin ... empty." She scratched at her hands absently. Then, she noticed a weird texture on her skin. Her hands were rough, almost like ... scales. Thin webbing had formed between the fingers of both hands. "What is this?"

Eric's eyes widened. "It's the eel spirit. You're beginning to transform."

Her eyes filled with fear. "I can't stay here. If I can't handle the desert as a human, there's no way ..."

His kiss silenced whatever she was about to say. He poured his energy into their connection, calling the hawk. It surged, but the presence of the eel was stronger. It had been neglected too long and needed nourishment to survive. Hawk or no hawk, she needed water.

Nancy swayed under the kiss. Eric's mind was a whirl of thoughts and feelings. He was worried about her, about failing her. He doubted himself and his ability to do as she'd asked and needed. The only time she'd felt this degree of torment within him was when they'd first been lost in the desert. He was at conflict with himself, torn between what he thought rationally and what he believed through faith.

The kiss ended and she looked at her hands. They were normal again, but she felt far from normal. Already, the effects were wearing off. She had minutes at best. Her chest burned with every ragged breath. Her skin itched and hurt. It was a strain to keep her eyes open. How much longer could she remain standing?

Silently, Eric repeated everything Nancy told him. She sensed him opening a portal. This was huge on many levels. That she accepted and believed in her own insight so readily was an incredible show of faith, and a good sign she was accepting her Calaspian nature. The intuition and insight of a newly forming Calaspian were not to be taken lightly. They tended to sense things more strongly than older Calaspians whose senses were dulled over the years. They took many things for granted, those that a new Calaspian would sense right away.

Of course, with practice came experience. Newer Calaspians may sense things more strongly, but they didn't always understand what they sensed. They could be wrong. Then again, a part of her had always been Calaspian. How did that contribute to everything?

Eric inhaled deeply and cleared his mind, starting over. Nancy said he could open a portal to Calaspia. She was absolutely sure about it. She also sensed his doubt. That was what she felt and what she believed. The question was, did he believe her? Did he trust her instincts enough to follow her on a leap of faith? This entire journey was a leap of faith for her. He knew she struggled constantly with accepting her new reality. Hers had not been a world of magic, shape-shifters, and travel between worlds. She adapted ... and amazingly well to her new life, accepting the crazy and impossible. A good bit of that was based simply on his word. He told her these things were possible, and she believed him. Now, she was asking him to believe her.

He thought back to the conversation in the church. She'd accused Calaspians of taking the easy road, of maintaining their faith only because they put themselves in a place where faith was easy and rarely tested. How strong was his faith? All he believed, he grew up with and witnessed to be true. When was the last time he was forced to have faith in something he was unsure about? Losing Nancy in the desert almost broke him. Seeing her weak and hurting was driving him mad with fear. Fear was the opposite of faith. Nancy showed more faith with each flight they took than he'd been forced to muster in his life. It was time he put aside his own fear and leapt, trusting and committing himself to whatever the outcome of that leap might be.

He felt the hawk spirit surge within, strengthened by faith. It was ready to soar and experience all the twists and turns life had in store. He couldn't remember the last time he felt so alive. As a Calaspian who prided himself on his faith, it was humbling to realize how weak his faith had truly been. He didn't know where the future would lead or where today would, but he was excited to find out. Eric's hands clasped hers. "If you believe it can be done, I'll trust you, just as I asked you to trust me," he said quietly.

"Really?" Their connection flashed with excitement and joy.

"Don't doubt your intuition. It's stronger than you know. You're also right in thinking your insights are tied to your breathing. When you align yourself with faith and hope, and trust your senses and instincts, it calls to your Calaspian nature. Both of them," he added. "The stronger your faith, the stronger your animal spirits will be, and the more you'll be influenced by them. It's a good thing."

"Except when you're stuck in a desert with a water animal inside of you," she pointed out.

"True," he agreed. "So, let's get you out of here.

CHAPTER THIRTEEN

Nancy smiled happily. He believed her. Eric didn't think she was crazy. He trusted her. It was a perfect moment followed by an intense feeling of foreboding. They were out of time. She and Eric were in danger. "He's here. He found me."

Anxiously, Eric looked around.

She didn't need to. She could feel the approaching beasts. Three lurked behind them and five others were scattered around. The house was on the edge of the city. There was only a thin line of trees between them and the beasts situated in the sand dunes. The man was farther behind them, moving steadily forward. She could see him in her mind.

Pressure filled her head. Her vision reduced to pinholes of light. The pain in her chest was intense. Dense energy swirled around. Escape. She needed to elude this pain, danger, and dry and barren land. She needed water. Oh, how she needed water. In the midst of everything, it was all she could think about. Cool, refreshing, life-giving water.

Her lungs burned. Her vision darkened and she felt herself falling.

Somewhere in the darkness, muted sounds and strange sensations surrounding her, she felt the banished man and beasts move farther away. Or was it she moving? She couldn't tell. Eric was near, caught up in the same energy that contained her. No ... *he* was the origin of the energy. Their emotions and thoughts were mingling and merging, feeding off each other. Her desire to escape and need for water added to his desire to protect her and the resolution to trust and have faith that he could open a portal, as she'd said he could.

Nancy gasped. She was no longer falling, but neither could she see. She felt as though she were floating, supported by a million plush pillows. Her skin tingled. The darkness moved around her and evolved into a faint glow that barely penetrated the shadows.

She moved her arm and felt resistance. Light encircled her, seemingly originating from her skin. It glistened. Her awed gaze traveled to her hands and the small webs of skin. The odd light floated around her body, as though she were under water. Only ... she could breathe.

Nancy spun until she located the light of the moon. Heading for that, she broke through the surface and found herself in the middle of a large lake. She was no longer in the sands of time. There were city lights and buildings in the distance. The sky swirled with amazing colors, but she could tell she was back on Earth. And she was swimming.

Nancy tipped her head back, moonlight beaming on her face. Tears of joy filled her eyes. This was a million times better than the best rainstorm. Tilting back farther, she sank her head into the water. Her body followed in a dive. She let her body make all the decisions as water embraced her. The peace was most welcome.

Her body was fast in the water, cutting through it with little resistance. Arms tucked tightly against her body, she turned and looped around. Her body was super flexible, bending in ways that would be impossible for a human. Diving deep, she shot up and jumped high out of the water. Floating for a few seconds in the air, it felt as if she were flying. Then, she was back in the inky depths of the mountain lake. Now that her eyes had adjusted, she was amazed by all she could see—glowing plants and shimmering rocks lining the lake bed. She explored, jumping high out of the water three more times, just to see how high she could reach. Her body had never felt this alive before. Energy levels elevated, she felt as if she could do anything.

Coming at last to shore, she climbed from the water onto a sandy beach. The air smelled of sage. In the moonlight, she examined her body. Small shiny scales glistened while thick webbing was clearly visible between her fingers and toes. Strange wisps of translucent skin hung around her elongated body. This felt perfect, natural, right.

Nancy stretched her senses, trying to find Eric. She could almost sense him, or at least she thought she could. Was this the same feeling that had led Eric to her at the church, and again in the sands? She closed her eyes and tried to pinpoint it, but the sense was too new. All she could tell for certain was he was close by.

———

ERIC WOKE up and rolled over on the wet stone floor. Water lapped his feet. It was dark, but he could see he was in some kind of cave. The mouth was narrow and jagged, and opened onto a large body of water. It was the only way out that he could see. Portal energy pulsed just under the surface of the water.

Unable to fly out the cave, he took on his human form and waded into the water. They were back on Earth. Extending his senses, he searched for Nancy, finding her quickly, but something was different. She seemed changed. Then, he sensed it—the eel spirit inside her had awakened. She was strong, rejuvenated, *alive*.

A shadowy form moved through the water with lightning speed and shot up into the air, twirling elegantly before re-entering the water headfirst. She was too far away to see well, and her form was very different, but he knew her nonetheless. Eric filled with elation, transfixed on Nancy's energetic display of agility. Her excitement would have been contagious even without their bond. She had him worried in the desert, but that was over now. She swam along the shore, beyond where he could see.

His Nancy, he mused. He wondered what it would have been like to live an entire life not knowing who he really was. Her stories of how difficult her life had been ran through his mind, and he felt her pain and confusion back in the desert. All of that was over now. Her soul sang with feelings of freedom and openness. For the first time, she was her true self; she was finally at peace with the animal spirit within.

Her mind clumsily searched for his. He smiled. She still had a lot to learn, but she was well on her way. In some ways, she'd surpassed him. He still couldn't believe he was able to open a portal, but Nancy had believed he could all along. Only, they weren't in Calaspia. How had he brought them back to Earth, a place he'd never been? It had to have been Nancy. Their emotions and thoughts had been wholly intertwined before they'd left the desert, her emotions intense. She'd been focused on going someplace safe with water she so desperately needed. This destination had to be her doing. ...He got them out of the desert; she brought them to this lake.

Reaching his mind out to hers, Eric helped her understand her senses and locate his presence. Something splashed nearby, and a dark shadow flew through the water toward him. She came up behind him and curled her arms around his chest, her face on his back.

He wasn't sure it was possible, but her emotions were significantly amplified. He took a deep breath to center himself. Opening his eyes, he turned to look at her, but she wouldn't let him. She clung to his back. "Let me see you," he chuckled.

"Uh, uh." Nervous how he'd react, her arms clenched him tighter.

Eric smiled, looking down at what he could see. Her arms and fingers were longer, covered in tiny black scales. He clasped her hand and turned it to get a better look. He'd seen eel demonics before, but never this closely. Bringing her hand to his mouth, he softly kissed her fingers. Her scales were wet and cool. Then, he kissed her hand and arm. Finally, she relaxed her hold enough that he could face her.

Still treading water, he took in her changed features. Her hair was slicked back and black, and her eyes shone with frosty, pale blue with flecks of sparkling white. Tiny scales ran along her cheekbones and down her neck, onto her shoulders. They continued down her arms and chest.

The scales were a mix of translucent white and dark black, reflecting a myriad of colors as bright moonlight shone on them. Her lips were pale, but not in an unhealthy way; no longer dry and cracked, they were full and moist. This was Nancy, *his* Nancy, and she was beautiful.

Eric kissed her with the full depth of his feelings. Her nervousness melted and she returned the kiss.

———

NANCY THREW herself into the kiss, wrapping elongated arms around Eric's body and holding him close. A shiver danced down her back, and the eel form melted away. Nancy struggled to remain above water, but Eric was there for her, holding her. She was human again, whatever that meant. She laughed to herself. She'd never be truly human again, and that was fine. Unfortunately, the human part of her still couldn't swim, but at least she wasn't afraid of the water anymore. That was something.

Holding onto rocks, Eric guided them to a small beach and helped her onto the ground before pulling himself ashore.

"Well, that was inconvenient timing. I hope that doesn't happen the next time I'm in the water."

Eric laughed. "You'll get the hang of it. Besides, I think that one was mostly my fault. I distracted you. I just couldn't resist." He kissed her again.

"Understandable." She giggled and stood up. "I wonder where we are."

Climbing the hill, she walked over rocky paths and patches of grass to find the summit. Spinning, she saw water on all sides. This was an island. By her feet was a strip of concrete, completely out of place. At one end was a little hole like one might find in miniature golf. "Ogapogo Island," she realized. She was in Canada, at Lake Okanagan. "This is where Adeline was found." Fascinated by the story as a child, she'd extensively researched the area.

"That makes sense. There was portal energy in one of the caves down there. But it's only accessible by water. That was probably where she came through."

"You found a portal?"

"I wouldn't say found so much as woke up next to," he corrected with a wry smile.

"I came here once for a trip a few years back, just to see this place." Funny to think she'd been so close to a portal to Eric's world. Looking back, she recalled how rejuvenating that trip had felt. She'd always wanted to return. It had been the one time she'd seriously wanted to swim. The lake had called to her. If she'd listened to her body back then, how different would her life had been? Maybe she'd have found the portal and met Eric sooner.

She stared at the lake, its smooth dark surface reflecting the colorful spectrum of Solstice magic lighting the sky. The water called to her still. A part of her wanted to run and jump off the top of the mountain into it. "Now that the eel spirit has fully emerged, its hold over you will be stronger for a time." Eric hugged her from behind. She leaned into his embrace, feeling a different kind of yearning, just as strong as the pull of the water. Where her eel power felt blue and cool, this energy felt yellow and hot. It was her hawk spirit, the spirit that tied her to Eric. She imagined two balls of light moving around inside of her, fighting for supremacy. Her dual affinity. Now that her body was fully hydrated and recharged, the hawk wanted its time.

Nancy felt a twinge of fear. Where the eel energy had felt natural, a part of her, this new energy was demanding.

Who would she be when all this was over? She wanted to run away, into the depths of the water. She wanted to disappear into the warmth of Eric's embrace. Tired of fighting, she wanted to surrender and go wherever the spirits took her.

"Breathe," Eric instructed softly, his lips close to her ear. "Don't be so hard on yourself. As far as I know, no one has ever had to accept two animal spirits at once."

"What about the other dual affinities you mentioned?"

"They're generally born with one animal and don't get the second until adulthood, when they're mated, or they inherit both from their parents and grow up with them from infancy."

"How do I accept the hawk without repressing the rest of me? Or do I constantly have to choose which part of myself I'm going to hold back? And what about my human side? How can it compete with these powerful spirits inside me?"

"It doesn't. My family, we aren't hawk or human. We're both, always."

She thought back to her eel transformation. That was how it had felt. But how could she be three things at once? "I can't think straight. Can we go back by the water for a bit?"

"Sure." He took her arm, leading the way down the hill.

The footing was trickier going down than coming up, especially with her bare feet. A stone pierced the arch of her foot. Her hand slipped from Eric's grip and she fell through a small cluster of bushes concealing a hole in the ground. She lost her sense of direction as murky darkness and flying dirt made it difficult to see. Finally, her body slid to a stop on cold stone. She coughed and pushed up with bruised hands and arms. She felt Eric's concern. "I'm okay," she said and coughed again.

"Hold on. I'll come down."

"No, wait," she called. "The hole is pretty tight in a couple spots. I'm not sure you could fit. Give me a sec." Squinting into the darkness, she looked around. "I see light up ahead." Crawling forward, she peered around the wall. The light was brighter. Eyes closed, she listened to the water lapping against rocks. "I think there's an opening to the beach or lake up ahead. I'll go that way and meet you outside."

"Okay."

She sensed Eric's uncertainty. "It'll be fine. You'll know if I need you," she assured him. His anxiety lessened.

Nancy half crawled, half walked through narrow tunnels. She kept moving, until the opening of the cave came into sight. Finally on the beach, she sighed and dusted off her hands. "Whew."

Unfortunately, she wasn't alone.

"Hello, Naitaka," a voice greeted from behind a nearby tree.

Nancy froze. She knew that voice and the growls that accompanied it. He'd found her.

"It's your darling, Gelick."

The eel and hawk fought within for control. Both wanted to protect her from this threat. The eel won, and her limbs, covered with scales, grew longer. She saw his eyes widen in shock.

"Just like her. You look just like her." His eyes clouded with memory. "My Naitaka. You've come back to me!"

She stepped away. "I'm not Adeline," she told him.

He shook his head. "So much like my sweet Adeline. We were going to have a life together. We could *still* have a wonderful life together, but you must stop visiting this lake, my Naitaka," he said, slipping further into his delusion. "I've told you it's dangerous. The humans fear you. They could hurt you. That's why I followed you through the under-water portal, to keep an eye on you, because I care about you. Everything I do is for you." He reached out to take her arm, but she sidestepped him.

His face flashed with anger. "You're not my Naitaka. You're an impostor. What have you done with my precious Adeline? How did you get her necklace? You're like her brother, trying to keep us apart, just because we aren't the same kind. I don't care if she's a water spirit and I'm land. We *can* be together."

"You're crazy! Adeline died hundreds of years ago, because you killed her brother."

"She's dead?"

His shocked and horrified expression sent off warning bells in her head. He was even more unstable than she'd thought. This guy was so all over the place, she couldn't read or judge what he'd say or do. There was probably a right way to talk to someone like him, but she had no idea what it was.

Gelick shook his head, appearing as if he'd hit upon something. A cut materialized on his cheek. He blinked several times and grief evolved into anger.

She tensed.

"*You*! You killed her and took her necklace. Then, you took her from me."

Nancy's eyes widened with fear. If there was a right way to deal with a crazy person, she'd obviously not done it. "I didn't kill her. She was my great, great ... uh, something or other grandmother. She died way before I was born."

"You killed her," he repeated. "Now, I'm going to kill you." Gelick changed into a panther and charged.

———

ERIC TRACKED Nancy's position from above ground. She'd taken several turns in and then out. He took a calming breath. She was safe for the moment, but they needed to get out of here. Then ... he felt her fear. She was in danger. He heard faraway voices. One sounded like Nancy's, but it was deeper. She was in her eel form.

"You killed her," the man said furiously. "Now, I'm going to kill you!"

Eric transformed to fly to her rescue and felt Nancy extend her senses when she recognized his nearby presence. Her desire to be by him was strong. And then, suddenly, she was beside him, having materialized out of thin air.

When he'd previously seen her in her eel form, most of her body had been hidden by water. This time, she was standing in full view, her body shimmering in the starlight. She was thinner and taller, close to his height; if he were in his human form, she might actually be a little taller.

She flinched and stepped back, anticipating an attack. She scanned the surroundings in confusion, noticed him and smiled with relief. "Eric!"

He was beside her in an instant.

"I thought of you, and then I was here. How did I do that?"

"I don't know." Eric hugged her tightly and felt her new arms around him. "But with you, very little surprises me."

Her deep eel voice said anxiously, "Gelick the panther, the banished, he's here. He's crazy. He thinks I'm Adeline ...

or I killed Adeline. He wasn't making any sense, but either way, he's really angry."

A roar rumbled across the island. Nancy clutched Eric's arms when the panther sprang through the trees and rushed at them. Glistening white teeth snarled and snapped. Pushing Nancy behind him, Eric caught the full force of the panther's attack. Eric grabbed him and they tumbled down the mountain.

———

NANCY WATCHED THEM FALL. The air shimmered and energy poured from Gelick. Flowers sprouted and died within seconds. A tree limb dissolved into dust. He was manipulating the flow of time.

Howls cried out behind. While she was focused on Eric and Gelick, two phantoms charged. She darted down the hill, stumbling over her long feet.

"Fish out of water," she mumbled. She tried to call the human or hawk sides, but her body wouldn't cooperate. Why was her body failing her? This eel form was useless. *She* was useless. Frustrated, she cried out.

Her arm screamed in pain. She expected to see blood or an injury, but her arm was fine. Confused and hurting, she fell. A beast in mid-jump sailed over her body. She rolled and scrambled upright, but every time she tried to use her arm, pain prevented it. It took several tries to get her feet back under her while avoiding attacking phantoms.

Thunder rocked the island as they neared. She struggled to remain ahead of the outstretched claws. Despite clumsy feet and an aching arm, she managed to put distance between herself and them. Pain stabbed her chest. Nancy fell again, struggling to breath. Her first thought was she was having a breathing attack, but this was more as if something had struck her.

Were some of the phantoms invisible? Where were these attacks coming from? Before she could figure it out, one of the creatures caught up and sank its teeth into her shoulder, and sucked on her life force energy. It wasn't taking chances with her this time. Razor-like teeth sank deeply into her flesh. Blood ran down her arm, but. She barely noticed. The pain of her energy being stolen was far greater.

In her mind, she screamed. What was wrong with her? She didn't need another body to fight back. She'd fight and survive no matter what form she took, because they were all part of her, and she refused to let things end like this. She had a life to look forward to, and these phantoms wouldn't steal that from her.

With a yell, she pushed and punched the beast in the face until he let go. Grabbing a long stick, she swung at the other three approaching beasts. She'd accumulated more pursuers along her run. She connected with one on the nose and scrambled up a ledge, then jumped and landed on one of them. Clawing at those nearby, she frightened some with her ferocity. Instinctively, she shouted "Kree-eee-ar" in various timbres. Fire burned in her soul. Her blood was a river of heated pulsing energy. Glancing at her hands, she saw talon-like fingers.

The more she fought, the stronger she felt. Claws and teeth ripped at her flesh. She fought on, her body exploding with energy. She was Nancy, descended of eel and Earth, mated to hawk. She refused to be felled by these pathetic, bottom-feeding shadows of wasted lives.

Feathers covered her shoulders, chest, and neck, and her feet and calves transformed to that of a hawk. She screamed with pain as her bones twisted and mutated The rest of her body remained scaly. Muscles shifted, grew and formed to accommodate wings. Pain ripped through her back as giant wings emerged. The feathers held the same translucent glow of her eel body. And, still, she fought.

Finally, the beasts backed away to seek weak prey. She no longer fit the description of feeble or frail. As one, they returned to their master. Taking to the sky, Nancy followed.

CHAPTER FOURTEEN

T he rocks were hard and unforgiving during their long fall, but there was no time to worry about that. The panther—Gelick, Nancy had called him—was intent on destruction. His teeth and claws struck Eric again and again.

Eric clutched a clawed foot before it could slash his throat, but that left him open to the panther's bite. Long fangs sank into his arm and clamped down, breaking through muscle and bone. Eric yelled, but didn't let go. Twisting, he slammed the panther's head into a large rock and rolled off to the side.

Cradling his injured arm, he rose onto his knees. The panther stumbled around, disoriented from the blow. He shook violently and changed into a man. Then, he locked wrath-filled eyes on Eric. The wind blew fiercely around them, too strong to fly in, so Eric switched back to human form, using the extra weight to help maintain his footing.

Energy gathered around the man. Thunder sounded loudly, followed by flashes of pink lightning, which struck the ground beside him. A small tree sprouted. The man was causing a time storm.

Taking advantage of the distraction, Gelick ran forward headfirst, hitting Eric hard in the chest and pushing him back. Eric felt the wind leave his lungs. Intense pain shot through his shoulder, only the pain wasn't from him; it was from Nancy. He was feeling her pain. She was injured.

He ducked, avoiding a powerful punch, and glanced at his arm. She'd have felt that. He had to defeat this madman quickly, with as little injury to himself as possible, and get to her.

Moving out of reach, he scanned his surroundings. Rain hung suspended in mid-air, then fell quickly and unevenly. Lightning flashed again. He was forced to move rapidly to avoid getting hit. Gelick glided back and began directing weather at a furious pace.

Eric did a decent job of avoiding the attacks. Suddenly, he was brought to his knees in pain; he felt it in his legs and back, as though his body were being ripped apart. His mind clouded, focus nonexistent. His body regained its hawk form. A powerful wind flung him against the trees and lightning struck his injured arm. Eric screamed, then watched in amazement as the blood ran *into* his wound, his bone resetting, the cut healing. His body still ached, but his arm had mended. The lightning had reversed time around the break. "Thanks," he said with appreciation.

Gelick yelled in anger. "You will *not* keep us apart!" He used the wind to propel a downed tree. Eric rolled and leapt upright despite the pain. He felt a surge of powerful energy from Nancy.

Blood stained Gelick's shirt. It originated from his chest, even though he'd not suffered hits to that area that Eric remembered. "Adeline is mine!"

Phantom beasts gathered nearby, engrossed in their battle.

"Adeline is dead," Eric shouted. "You're the one responsible."

"Lies. Adeline is alive. I've seen her. You won't keep her from me with your lies." Rocks, sticks, and branches flew at Eric.

He shielded his face and pulled in his wings to protect them.

"Eric!" Nancy called urgently from above.

Eric looked up to see Gelick charging in panther form. He used more projectiles as cover for his attack. He side-stepped Gelick and slashed the panther's face with taloned claws.

Gelick roared and snapped his teeth, catching Eric in the side. Eric spread his wings enough that he could move out of reach. He landed a firm kick in the panther's back. Springing into the sky, he struck again, this time flying into Gelick's side.

Gelick slipped and hit a felled tree. His yell began as a roar and ended as a human scream; his body transformed back into that of a man. A tree limb protruded from his chest where blood had appeared earlier. Gelick gazed down in confusion.

The weather intensified, wind howling, lighting striking, thunder booming. A shadow in the sky wavered and fell. Nancy. She was flying, but the wind was too strong for her to maintain her position. She plunged into the trees below.

Lightning struck the tree that impaled Gelick. It split, the top half flying off in a shower of fire and light. The entire island exploded into a blaze of lightning and swirling winds, time fluctuations happening at random. A tree burst from the ground and sprang up ten feet, covered in ripened fruit. Wind blew much of it to the ground, where in rotted in seconds. Time phantoms howled and raced from the center of the storm, only to be caught up in the winds and torn into ribbons, dark shadows no longer alive.

Eric flew straight to where Nancy fell. There, he found her curled on the ground, stunned, with only one visible injury on her shoulder. He swooped and grabbed her, and flew them out of danger. He could distinguish outlines of remaining phantoms, the stronger ones, running to the tree.

Gelick screamed as the phantoms took advantage of the easy meal his impaled body provided. They sucked at his life energy. Piercing shrieks of agony filled the night.

Landing on a nearby mountain peak, Eric held Nancy until the storm subsided and Gelick's screams were no more.

Looking at Nancy, he smiled in amazement. She was the most stunning vision of beauty and grace he'd ever seen. She was covered in the typical brown feathers of a red-tailed hawk, but there was a scattering of black and gray feathers throughout. Her body transitioned from feathers to shiny black scales, to porcelain-pale human skin. Her eyes were a pale violet with specks of white and red. Normally, at any given time, Calaspians with multiple affinities took on one or the other. It took a tremendous amount of acceptance throughout to reconcile the differences of their multiple animals and make them work in concert to create a full hybrid form. In fact, it could take hundreds of years to reach that point. Nancy had achieved it with her first hawk transformation. He couldn't believe how lucky he was to be mated to such a beautiful being.

Her lips curled upward slightly. "I'm glad you approve

of my appearance," she repeated his earlier words. Leaning close, she teased, "You should mind your thoughts."

"How about I just show you what I'm thinking instead?" He kissed her and, thinking of home, felt that now familiar shift of energy as they traveled to another world.

She looked around as far as she could. "Where are we?"

"Calaspia," he whispered.

"You brought us here, without a portal?" she smiled.

He nodded. "Turns out, it's not that hard if you have a little faith."

She leaned her head against him. Her cheek caressed his arm. Relaxing effortlessly into her eel body, she hugged him back. They settled in like that, blissfully content in each other's presence. Hawk and eel, so different, and yet, completely right. Solstice magic continued to cast a dazzling glow. They were finally alone, with no dangers or pressing needs to attend. It was the two of them, as it should be.

She stroked the small cuts and scrapes on his arm. "Did you get these when you fell down the mountain?"

"Yes. The one downside to matings: shared pain."

She looked at her shoulder. "Then you felt—"

"When you transformed," he confirmed. "Initial transformations can be difficult on a body not born with the animal spirit. Your body has to learn to make the change."

"Not born with it? Is that why the eel transformation didn't hurt?"

"Yes, and the future hawk transformation shouldn't cause any pain, either." He thought of her, in full hybrid form, flying high in the sky.

"I have no idea how I did that ... flying," she clarified. "It was just—"

"Instincts," he finished for her, impressed how well she read his thoughts.

Nancy ran fingers along a jagged cut. At her touch, it healed. She stared in wonder. "How—"

"You're a water affinity," he said casually, as though that explained anything. Eric laughed upon seeing her blank expression. "Water affinities often have healing abilities. Actually," he looked thoughtful, "I think you healed me before, up in the tree, when you fell asleep on me. I thought my shoulder healed a little quicker than usual, but I chalked it up to the Solstice time shift and forgot about it."

"Can I heal myself like that?"

Eric shrugged. "Give it a try."

Nancy hesitantly touched her shoulder. He felt her focus and energy gather. Her eyes closed and light surrounded her webbed fingers and moved into her shoulder. Slowly, the skin mended without a sign of injury. The light faded and she opened her eyes. "Cool," she smiled.

Without another word, she kissed him. There was no more need to speak. They sensed what the other was feeling. Pressing her onto the grass, he ravished her body with kisses.

"Change," he whispered into an ear. "Show me your hawk form."

Her eyes, hazel hawk eyes, shot open. A shiver skipped through her body. This time, the transformation was entirely that of the hawk. How different she looked with hazel eyes and brown feathers covering her head and face. As strange as it was, it suited her. Eric touched her face lovingly. "Just when I think you can't get any more beautiful, you prove me wrong."

Eric stood and pulled Nancy to her feet.

"What are you doing?" Her hawk eyes displayed passion.

He pulled her to him possessively and kissed the base of

her neck. "I'm going to make crazy ... " he kissed under her ear, "passionate ..." another kiss on her feathered cheek, " mind-blowing love to you." Holding her securely, they soared into the sky.

———

HER KNUCKLES WHITE, and feeling dizzy, Nancy tucked her head into this chest and held on tightly. She was unable to tell which way was up or how far they'd flown. He was moving quickly, this much she realized, but she was too afraid to open her eyes to see just how quickly.

Their movements slowed. "Look," he coaxed her.

Whimpering, she peeked from the corner of one eye. In the distance jammed with treetops and rivers, she saw a beautiful building atop a large hill; it sparkled with light.

"That's the temple," Eric explained. "That light's the power of the Solstice ritual, the magic that brought us together."

Forgetting the height and her fear, she kissed him. This felt right ... and perfect. His hands roamed her body, the claws raking her skin. Realization dawned and she wondered—if his hands were moving so freely and no longer holding her—why wasn't she falling?

Ending the kiss, she opened her eyes and panicked. She was flying, instinctually, like before. Only now that she was aware of what she was doing, she had no idea *how* she was doing it. Reaching out frantically, she clung to Eric.

Eric chuckled and held her close, flying up higher. Pulling in his wings, he began to freefall. Nancy cried out in surprise and fear. His gaze and mental connection beckoned her to trust him. When she nodded, he took her hands and stretched them out. Her eyes widened; without his hands around her, she felt even more afraid.

"Stretch your wings," he instructed. She hesitated and then did as he'd said. He extended his own wings at that same instant.

The wind caught their wings, halting their descent a few feet from a treetop. They continued like that, flying and falling, until they finally joined, their mating completed mid-air.

The connection had heightened every sensation. With air rushing past, an unfamiliar body and fresh senses, and the excitement of giving in to desire, Nancy didn't know of any experience that could be more intense.

When it was over, he didn't let go and, with expert skill, led them back up in an exciting swirl of flight.

Euphoria overtook her, and she kissed him again. Closing her eyes, they freefell again. She was no longer afraid. She could tell the moment his wings stretched forth and extended her own.

Wind currents pulled them apart, and she found herself flying solo. Leaning into a glide, she soared over a forest. Nancy looked everywhere, awed by how sharp her vision was. What she saw in the boat back in the desert was nothing compared to the colors and lights here. She'd thought this place beautiful before, but it was even more so now. The wind blowing against her face and through her feathers was as soothing as the best rainstorm. She couldn't believe she'd lived her entire life without knowing what this was like.

Eric approached her side, giving her just enough room to move her wings. She thought that moment would last forever, but then the wind shifted. Inexperienced with flying, the sudden change sent her tumbling, but Eric was on her in an instant, as though he'd anticipated the change.

He set them down on the upper limbs of a nearby tree. Nancy held on to the trunk and tried to catch her breath. Her heart still beat quickly from the excitement.

"Not bad for your first full flight." He walked gracefully onto the next limb.

"I can't believe I just did that. I'm going to pass out now."

Eric laughed and jumped to another limb. He looked downright giddy. Nancy gazed around and wished she hadn't. They had to be hundreds of feet above the ground. Her head spun with vertigo and she clutched the trunk tighter. The limb she was on sank. Immediately, she felt Eric's arm around her.

"Are you alright?"

"It's just a little high up here."

Eric laughed again. "You were just a lot higher."

"I never claimed to make sense. Besides," she added, "you were providing a bit of a distraction up there."

"Hmm," he snuggled up close. "I can distract you here, if you like."

The night sky, peaceful and serene, shone with a million bright stars. The brightness from before was gone. "Why does everything look so different?" she asked.

Eric nibbled her ear. "We're back in regular time, my dear little bird."

"I thought we had to make it to the temple to get back."

"As I said, Solstice magic is unpredictable. When the bond is strong enough, unusual things can happen."

It was complete. She was joined to Eric forever. The thought brought excitement and nervousness. Just like flying. She'd never thought anyone could accept her as completely as Eric did. She was beyond strange, straddling the three worlds of land, air, and sea. A hawk afraid to fly, an eel afraid to swim. That he wanted to be with someone like her seemed incredible. That she could be destined to love someone and be loved by someone as brave, selfless, and kind as he brought feelings of intense gratitude. She was blessed beyond her wildest dreams.

"I'll teach you all I know of the hawk," he promised softly, sensing her train of thought. "And there are many extended families of Adeline to teach you all about your water affinity." He tucked her hair behind an ear and smiled lovingly. They kissed.

Both pulled away as energy started building around Calaspia. "What is that?" she asked, perplexed.

Eric narrowed his eyes. "It couldn't be." Then, he grinned. "Things are about to get interesting. The other couples caught up in Solstice are returning. Whenever you're ready, we can fly to the temple. That's where everyone else will be going. It's where the celebrations are held. I can carry you if you like," he offered.

"I'm okay, I think, maybe. Don't go too far."

He chuckled. "I'm right beside you. Follow me."

"Eric," she pressed his arm to stop him. "I ... I know you can feel what I feel, and with the mating complete this may seem redundant, but I just want to say ..." She touched his face. "I just want to say, I absolutely love you with my entire heart and being. I accept our mating without reservation and without fear. I want to be with you and only you for all eternity."

"Nancy," his voice choked with emotion. "My Nancy, my love, I'll love you forever. You've taught me more about faith and bravery than I've learned in centuries on my own. My entire life before this was preparation for you. I accept every unique and amazing part of you, to be my mate and partner."

They kissed, sealing their promises, and stood in silent appreciation for the magnitude of the moment. Then, he smiled and stepped back. She watched him leap from the limb and fall before spreading his wings, and circling around to wait for her. Watching him fly was a beautiful sight.

With a deep breath, Nancy took a step, paused, and jumped before she could think about it. Despite her best efforts, she heard herself yelp as she fell. Then, her wings spread on their own and she began to fly. Eric waited a few seconds for her to steady herself, and then led the way. Together, they flew to the temple.

CHAPTER FIFTEEN

"Where are Eric and Ephraim?" Narlic asked. He put down an armful of food dishes carefully on the banquet table next to the others he'd brought before, and wiped a hand over his brow.

Their mom, Evelynne, laughed. "I'm sure they'll be here soon."

"Sure, just in time to eat everything," he groused.

She gave him a kiss on the cheek and smiled. "Thank you for all your help bringing the food down here. I couldn't have managed it without you. All my other children are too busy with their new babies and children this year. Young families ..." She sighed contentedly.

"Not a problem. I just don't understand why you wanted to bring the food down here instead of celebrating at home like you usually do."

"Every Solstice is special, a time of promises and renewal, a time of hope and thankfulness for our many continued blessings. And this year is even more special. I got the same feeling the day I was mated, and the day each of my other children found their mates."

Suddenly, she spun around, exuberant eyes eagerly looking everywhere. Before he could ask what she felt, he felt it, too. Powerful energy swirled around them, coalescing in certain spots.

All at once, couples appeared around the temple grounds, entering from swirling spots of portal energy. Some were human forms. Some took hybrid or full animal forms. Some were a mix of hybrids or animals leading humans. Smiling men and women pointed and described the surroundings. Happy family members and friends ran up to meet the new mates. Sensing the arrivals, Calaspians ran and flew in from all directions. Within moments, the entire field was bustling with excitement.

Narlic's eyes widened with wonder. With a confident declaration, she put a voice to his thoughts. "The portals to Earth are reopening."

————

"SO, you really didn't see a single phantom beast? Eric asked, disappointed.

"No," his brother answered. "But I did almost die of blood loss and a pretty bad head injury, if that makes you feel any better."

They looked at each other and said in unison, "Don't tell Mom." Laughing, they nodded knowingly.

"It's a good thing your mate is a doctor," Eric commented.

"Yes, I guess, even though she didn't inherit the eel spirit like your mate, she still developed the desire to heal her own way."

Eric watched Nancy talk excitedly with her sister, both in human form, standing under a tree by the water. Her joy was intense. Eric grinned. Nancy still didn't have any shoes on. Beside him, Ephraim looked longingly at his new mate. Eric clapped a hand on his brother's shoulder and laughed. "There'll be plenty of time for that later, brother. Let's go find mom's pie before it's gone."

That snapped Ephraim out of his daze. "Absolutely. I'm starved."

Eric laughed, and they walked through the crowd.

The celebration was in full swing. While there was always music and dancing at Solstice, this year was particularly energetic. He couldn't remember the last time this many people had come out. Most families put in an appearance at the festival, but spent most of the time celebrating in private at home. Not this time. There were Calaspians from far-away forests, islands, and boroughs. Everyone was congregated in this one spot. Angelics and demonics ran around in animal, human, and hybrid forms. People drank and ate. Couples danced. Brothers traded shoulder punches and congratulatory handshakes. Sisters and friends laughed, cried, and hugged. There was something happening everywhere. It took them some time to navigate their way through it all and find their mom's table.

"My boys!" Their mom grabbed them both in a big hug. "Where are my new daughters?" She handed them plates of pie.

"Over there," Eric motioned. "Turns out, our mates are sisters. They had a lot to talk about."

"Mom, you'll never believe it," Ephraim said. "They're both from ..."

"Earth, I know," she interrupted. "All the mates this year are!"

"All of them?" Eric asked in surprise. He knew there

were quite a few new faces he didn't recognize, but he hadn't realized they were all from Earth.

"All of them," she beamed happily.

"That's why all the old portals opened," Eric observed.

"Yes," she said excitedly. "Our worlds are reconnected!"

"That's great, Mom." Ephraim put down his empty plate, hugged his mom, and reached for another piece of pie.

A crew of hawk hybrids walked up with a flock of children, running, jumping, skipping, flying, and climbing on everything and everyone. They gathered around Eric and Ephraim in a series of hugs and congratulations. Kisses on the cheek came from his brothers' wives. "What are you guys doing here?" Eric asked.

"Did you think we'd miss meeting our new sisters?" Ethan asked.

"Mom said she wouldn't babysit for the next year if we didn't come," Elijah said dryly, bouncing Evee on his hip. His wife punched his arm. "What?" he asked innocently. "I wanted to sleep. We could always meet the mates tomorrow, when it's daytime."

Eric laughed. Jean ran up and jumped on Eric for a hug. He lifted her into his arms and hugged her tightly.

"Mommy said we have new aunts."

"You sure do," he answered. Pointing, he leaned close. "You see those two over there, by the lake?"

She nodded and smiled. "They're pretty."

Eagan whistled. "Not bad." It was his wife's turn to hit him. He shrugged. "Of course, they're not as pretty as you, dear." She smiled and hugged his arm. Eagan looked back at Eric and Ephraim, and mouthed, "Wow."

Ephraim choked back a laugh as Eagan's wife looked at

him suspiciously, but he offered an innocent look in response.

"Come on, girls," their mom said, gathering her sons' daughters and children. "Let's go introduce ourselves."

Eric smiled and watched the women head to the lake. His brothers laughed and said something teasingly to Ephraim, but he was too busy working his way through the food to care.

"Make room," their father called, carrying an armful of food to the table.

Eric laughed and grabbed some dishes, while he brothers stepped in to help with the rest. "How much did Mom cook?" he asked. "Is there more?"

"No, this is the last of it. Narlic and I have been carrying it down here for the past hour. We were done, but then the portals opened and your mother flew back home to throw together a few more things. I don't think there's a speck of food left in our entire house." Smiling, he shook his head and pulled Eric and Ephraim into a big hug. Ephraim grunted uncomfortably and slipped out to get food from the new trays.

"Are you injured?" their father asked.

"Nah, I'm fine ... ow!" He cringed as their father pushed Ephraim's side.

"Hmm, that's why there's dried blood in your hair."

"Having trouble with the mate, already?" Eagan teased. "I guess I can see it. She's way out of your league."

Ephraim threw a roll at Eagan, who dodged it easily. "I'm fine," he turned back to his dad. "I took a fall in the howling caves. As fate would have it, my mate is a doctor of sorts, so she patched me up."

Elijah grinned. "I bet she did."

Ethan laughed and elbowed Elijah's arm playfully. "Oh, it hurts here and there. Please use your healing touch."

"But be gentle," Elijah joked.

Ephraim threw two more rolls, hitting one in the head and the other in the chest. They laughed heartily in response.

Eric chuckled and looked at his father. "Where is Narlic, anyway?"

"Not sure. I told him I had the last load of food, so he could go enjoy the festival. I'm sure he's around somewhere."

Looking around with senses as well as eyes, Eric found Narlic on the outskirts of the festival grounds. Excusing himself, he headed that way.

Narlic sat on a small hill near the water. While some parts of the lake were active with aquatic Calaspians and excited humans, this area was quiet and calm. Turning away from the party, he began to casually toss pebbles.

Eric walked up beside him and leaned against a tree. "Looks like you found the best spot."

Narlic grinned. "You know I don't really do crowds of people. Congratulations. I know the wait was starting to wear you down."

"It was worth it."

Narlic stared back at the lake. "I'm glad. Just ... promise you'll be careful. I know your mates will probably want to travel back and forth to Earth. Now that the portals are open, and with so many Earth mates, I'm sure there'll be a lot of that again ... and, well, you just can't be too careful."

Eric sat down beside his friend and placed a hand on his arm. "If it makes you feel better, to get back here, Nancy and I had to face a fairly powerful banished controlling an army of phantoms. We were separated and got lost in the sands of time, and I had to learn to travel between the realms without a portal. And turns out Nancy is descended from a fallen eel demonic, so she was basically suffocating from lack of water a good bit of the time." Eric laughed at Narlic's shocked, wide-eyed expression.

Narlic looked thoughtfully back at the water. "You know what, that *does* make me feel better. Still."

"We'll be careful."

"Good. I don't want to lose any more family."

Eric smiled and clapped him on the shoulder. "You got it, brother. Now, I should go find my mate."

Narlic nodded and Eric walked back to the party.

———

CONGRATULATIONS WERE OFFERED EVERYWHERE. Strangers embraced Nancy and offered well wishes like long-time friends and family. Some of them could truly be family, she thought. It was amazing to feel so welcome and accepted. It was also a little overwhelming. Names and faces became a blur. Cindy had long been swallowed up by the crowds. She was always better than Nancy at accepting attention and mingling in large groups of people. She itched to break free, stretch her wings, literally and figuratively, and explore her eel side a little more. Dozens of animal instincts were coursing through her, aching to be freed.

Warm arms wrapped her from behind. "How are you doing, my little bird?"

She laughed happily. "You know, I think that name is growing on me."

"Good." He nuzzled her neck. "Are you having a good time?"

"Yeah. It's a little crazy how friendly everyone is. I don't think I've ever talked to so many people in one day. But yeah, it's good. I met your mom and your brothers' wives. One of them gave me shoes." She held out a foot clad in soft fabric with a solid yet comfortable sole. "These are so much better than my old ones."

"Ethan's mate, Lacy, makes those. They have healing plants woven in, so every time you walk, oils seep out and soothe the feet. They're very popular."

"I can see why." She sighed contentedly and leaned against Eric's chest.

Eric inhaled her scent and sighed, hugging her tightly. "I have something for you. I thought you might be hungry." Eric reached behind him and picked up a plate.

Nancy felt her jaw drop. On the plate was a piece of bread, no crust, with peanut-butter and a heart drawn on top. "You're kidding. You remembered that?" She threw her arms around his neck and kissed him. She grinned and took a bite of the bread. "Mmmm, that is really good peanut-butter. You know, you never told me any of your annoying habits."

He continued to hold her and stare lovingly as she ate. "You never asked. I believe you said they weren't important."

"I did not," she smiled, covering her mouth, so she could finish chewing. "I thought it, but I didn't say it."

"My mistake." He took the empty plate and set it down without looking away. Then, he kissed her deeply. "Mmmm, you're right. It is good. Are you up for a quick flight? I have something I'd like to show you."

"Absolutely." She transformed instantly, with speed and ease she'd not have thought possible a while earlier, and took to the sky. Eric flew up beside her and led the way deep into a forest, to a secluded grove. Nancy landed gracefully and looked around in awe. "This is beautiful!" Butterflies fluttered everywhere, eliciting a giggle.

Eric came up behind and pointed ahead. "This tree line marks the edge of an expansive forest. These trees are thousands of years old. Just over that hill you'll find the majority of avian settlements. And over there," he pointed to a stream, "is an inlet to that." He pulled back branches to reveal a large ocean.

Nancy pushed past. Water stretched as far as she could see. The sunrise on the horizon cast an array of pinks and blues across the sky. "Amazing."

"That," Eric continued, "is the domain of the aquatic Calaspians. They live in the ocean and connecting lakes and rivers, as well as the hundreds of islands dotting the water's surface. Underneath us are a series of caves, both above ground and underwater. Rivers travel underground all around here. This spot right here is on the edge of two worlds."

"Like me," she whispered.

"Look over there." He pointed behind, to a tree by a waterfall.

Nancy squinted. "Is that a house?" She jumped into the air and flew. Eric joined her. "It's something I've been working on for a few years. There are still finishing touches that need to be done, but it's mostly there."

She regarded the expert woodwork. "You built this?" she asked, impressed.

Eric opened the door and waited for her to enter. Nancy walked in and stopped in amazement. "You have furniture!" She spun around to take in everything at once. Placing a hand on the back of a chair, she admired the design. "Did you do this, too?"

"Alas, I cannot take credit for that. Ephraim helped me with the furniture. He has quite a skill."

Nancy arched an eyebrow in surprise. "I thought you lived on tree limbs."

Eric smiled. "Some do, but remember, my mother was human. My father has always tried to make our home as comfortable as possible for her. It's what Ephraim and I grew up with, so it's what we are most comfortable with."

"This place, all of it ... I don't have enough adjectives to describe how incredible it all is."

"There's one more thing." He grinned.

"What else could you possibly have to show me?" She laughed.

"One more thing," he winked and took her hand to lead her up the stairs to the bedroom loft. Nancy grinned, but Eric led them past the bed to a window overlooking a balcony. Nancy stepped through the small opening and onto the deck. "Now, stand over by the edge."

Nancy followed his instructions. The view was spectacular. She could see the ocean and sunset. Tree vines, covered in flowers, twined everywhere. The sound of the waterfall was peaceful. She closed her eyes and felt the mist from the falls cover her skin.

"Oh, wow!" She turned to the mist and let it spray her face. "This is perfect."

Eric walked up behind and wrapped arms around her. "I never understood what drew me here, why I felt compelled to build here, until I met you."

She turned and threw her arms around his neck, crossing her hands behind his head. At a loss for words, emotion swelling deep within, she kissed him. This magical home and this strong, wonderful man were hers. She spoke the only words she could think of to convey all she felt. "I love you."

Eric's eyes glistened with tears.

"I wish I could give you something even half as great as all you've given me."

"You gave me *you*. And one day, you'll bear our children. Those gifts are far greater than anything I can give you, but I'll spend the rest of eternity trying to come close. I love you, my little bird."

They kissed.

Eric pulled back and grinned. "Why don't we finish the tour? I believe you were curious about something in the loft. Shall we examine it more closely?"

Nancy grinned. "Absolutely."

EPILOGUE

Nancy stood with her feet on the upper limb of a giant, thousand-year-old sequoia. Her hand rested casually against the trunk. Despite the swaying of the tree, she no longer felt dizzy from the height. Stretching her wings, she bounded off, twirling through trees into the open air. Eyes closed, she glided, letting the wind tickle her face. Then, she somersaulted and transformed, shedding her hawk form.

Air rushed against her during a freefall. The old her would have cried out in fear, but the new her was exhilarated. With only a short distance to go, she emerged into her eel form. The cool dry air became warm, soothing water. A tiny splash announced her entrance into the lake, prompting a half-dozen eel demonics to swim around and smile in greeting. The others would arrive shortly. Her family. Her ancestors' family. Many knew Adeline directly. The rest knew her story and were more than thrilled welcome Nancy to their world.

She saw a shadow over the water and surfaced to see Cindy flying overhead. "Come on in," she called.

Cindy looked down and smiled. Her hawk coloring was very similar to Ephraim's.

With a laugh, she shook her head and landed on a rock near the shore.

Nancy swam over, circling the rock.

"Nice try," Cindy said, "but unlike you, I still can't swim."

"So, shed those wings and give it a try. I'll help."

Several heads popped out of the water as other eels came to see whom she was talking to. Once they saw Cindy, they smiled and waved, and returned to the water.

"No thanks," Cindy said. "You go and have fun. I'll let you attempt to drown me, er, I mean, try to teach me to swim later."

Nancy splashed her sister for good measure and leaned into crossed arms on the rock. "How did your visit with Mom and Dad go?"

"Good. They want to visit us after the babies are born." She touched her barely showing belly. "They're planning to come to Canada for a week to stay near the house."

"I'm glad you thought about getting that place." It had been Cindy's idea to tell their parents they'd taken a trip to where their family was from in an attempt to help Nancy's breathing problems, which worked. As a result, they'd decided to relocate there, met two brothers, fell in love, and got married after whirlwind romances.

Their parents were so glad that she could breathe, they weren't upset at the two for moving so suddenly. Nancy and Cindy pooled their savings and bought a small property with two bedrooms, big enough that the four of them could live there. It was far enough away that they didn't have to worry about unexpected pop-in visits. "They'll have to wait until after the Celebrations of the First-Borns."

Since most couples met through the mating rituals of Solstice, and all matings resulted in pregnancies, there was an abundance of people all over Calaspia born within a week or so of each other. Some children were born throughout the year, but most of the first-borns were born during that time. Never ones to ignore a good excuse for a celebration, they designated that week a festival.

"Don't worry. I told them to wait until we call when the babies arrive, so they don't have to worry about the babies arriving late and them having to go home without seeing them. I also gave them the wrong due date, two weeks later, just in case they felt like surprising us. Dad only gets the one week off, so we should be good."

"Sounds good." Nancy pushed off and swam out into deeper water. "I'm off. Later," she called and waved before submerging again. She'd join Cindy later. Eric and Ephraim were preparing dinner with their family and friends for later in the evening. There were many new things to learn and see, and she was no longer afraid. This was going to be fun. With a smile, she touched her rounding belly and swam off to rejoin the others.

ABOUT THE AUTHOR

"What do you want to be?"

When I was little, I answered that question with actor, writer, artist, astronaut, singer, fashion designer, and a few other things. Adults would grin at my answer and say I hadn't made up my mind yet. I told them, "No, I want to be all of them."

I never understood the idea of limiting yourself to one thing. Life is so big. There is room for many adventures.

As I grew, I continued to draw. I wrote and performed songs at talent shows. I drew designs for clothing and even sewed some outfits. I made my own wedding dress by hand. I studied digital design and learned to do some basic work in photo programs. Friends will tell you, I'm always jumping from one crazy project to another.

Again and again I've been told what I was doing was too difficult, I didn't know enough, I could never do it. And every time I've plunged headfirst into whatever my passion was driving me towards, with a near unwavering faith that I could do anything I put my mind to. People always want to tell you what you can't do. We are all capable of incredible things when we have faith and believe in ourselves. You may not succeed at everything you do, but you will never succeed at something you do not try.

Despite my vast array of different interests, writing has long held a special place in my soul. When I was twelve years old, I spent an entire summer writing a story. I often started projects without finishing them, before. This was different. I wrote every day. I wrote in the car, my room, and the laundromat. I wrote until, just as vacation was coming to an end, my story was done. I finished it. I knew in that moment, this was my calling in life. This was what I was meant to do.

From that moment on, I studied and wrote. Teachers and siblings told me to pursue a more practical career. I ignored them and followed my instincts.

When I needed a break, I still had all my other creative projects to help me recharge and have time to think. But I always returned to writing.

Through college, meeting and marrying my soulmate, working through jobs I hated, becoming mother to three wonderful boys, and homeschooling those same rambunctious boys, there have been challenges,. There were times I've had to take a break from regular writing to care for newborns and sick children. Though, even when I wasn't actively putting pen to paper (yes, I still use good old-fashioned notebooks and handwriting much of the time), my books are always somewhere in my mind. I've spent many nights crouched over paper, using the dim light from my phone or a night light to see enough to put down my thoughts, while my children sleep a few feet away. Writing is who I am.

My passion is in paranormal romances and fantasy books. I love writing about werewolves, and other shape shifters. I've also written about psychics.

I began writing fantasy after I was married. My husband and I used to get together with friends to play Dungeons & Dragons every Saturday. My husband wanted to create his own world with his own campaigns, so he enlisted my help in writing the background stories. He told me what his world was like, and some of the key players, and asked me to write backgrounds on other characters. I told him what I had, and he added content or made changes to fit his vision. It was a lot of fun to work on this with him.

Later, I was looking for a quick project to write for NaNoWriMo (National Novel Writing Month) and decided to put some of our notes into a full story of its own. That was the birth of our first collaborative fantasy book project.

It is great to be able to share something that is such a big part of my soul with my husband. He has always supported my writing. Even when it hasn't paid off financially, he has never once asked me to stop.

I don't know what the future holds, but I know this is what I'm called to do.

Lightning Source UK Ltd.
Milton Keynes UK
UKHW020650130920
369780UK00012B/475